Abou

Born in South Yorkshire ~~~~~ in 1988, Katie Suzanne Dryden has spent many years travelling abroad, exploring different cultures and listening to people's life stories along the way. One of the key fundamentals that captivated her in doing so was the fear that so many people seem to share of speaking out about their inner battles with themselves, their feelings of inadequacy, of not being able to handle pressure, their struggle to fit in with others and society as a whole – for these are in fact some of the key things that connects us as human beings. As someone who has fought intensely with her own mental health as well as witnessed its harmful effects upon others, the author's hope is that: *When East Meets West* will reach out to those people, raise awareness of the invisible illnesses that consumes far too many of us and finally create further understanding on what it really means to live with a mental disorder. She states that as individuals we need to be able to communicate these things to one another. We need to stop hiding behind closed doors and fake smiles. It's all about 'connecting' with others, whether it's through spoken words, painted or photographic images, simple gestures – or perhaps through the pages of a book.

Also available by Katie Suzanne Dryden is:
Sand in Soho Square.

Dedication

This dedication is split four ways and is for those that have helped me (and continue to do so) in putting the pieces back together.

For Ruth, whose kind words and stories not only made my days bearable, but also quite magical.

Vikkie, for being there and for staying, for supporting me in so many areas and for continuing to make me smile.

Pauline, for teaching me 'the skills' and for your warmth but most of all for being endlessly patient with me, which I know is a challenge.

Kirsten, thank you for sharing your light, your positivity and for giving me space to laugh and to cry.

Acknowledgments

A huge thank you to everyone at Austin Macauley Publishing for your gentle guidance, careful editing and most of all for being extremely supportive throughout.

Chapter One

White walls surround me, evoking anxious thoughts of medicine and doctors, which unsteadies me further. The ceiling is white, the row of three basins fixed within a sleek, marble top is white, and even the cool tiles beneath my feet are a fluorescent white, which, I notice as I look down, are so sanitised, iridescent, and sparkling that they reflect everything within this small confinement, made even smaller by the swarms of women entering and departing constantly. Stepping around me as I analyse everything, they go about their business, in and out again. Everyone is moving at a different pace, just like in the depth of life itself. It doesn't matter how fast we move, just as long as we are in fact *moving*; I read that somewhere, and instantly it was ingrained within me, always resurfacing at appropriate moments. I like reading other peoples' words, but I love *writing my own* even more. Once, after drinking far too much white wine and smoking incessantly, I managed to somehow fall asleep in a bathroom much like this one, and, when I woke up, all that whiteness drove me into a whirl of dizziness – a surreal haze. I had felt blind at first, and found myself contemplating whether or not I had died and perhaps, on a more hopeful level, ascended to heaven. It was an interesting and strangely comforting experience, I seem to recall, though, when I awoke from it, I took a mental note that I needed to lower my alcohol intake – to spend less time in the bathroom, and more time in the 'real' world, amongst people with more 'normal' worries, such as passing their driving tests, or not burning the chicken. Unfortunately, I'm not there yet – not by a long shot. This I know, and live with daily. To be completely honest, I find that I lose myself in thought quite often these days, and in the strangest of places: like bathrooms, for instance.

I was advised to try to write down my thoughts – to keep a sort of diary of what is going on, so that hopefully, when I am struggling, this might act as a kind of *coping mechanism*. I've followed the advice, though I'm not sure it has helped me cope any better. My own, somewhat sadistic, coping methods to this day remain, leaving a sort of map of my feelings all over my body; yet, it is a map that doesn't lead anywhere, except right back to the start, I guess.

Thoughts are interesting notions, aren't they? They come and go, like a light breeze passing through a quiet scene. Some are a little stronger, and I suppose could be more accurately described as a 'gusty wind', or a 'hurricane', perhaps. Sometimes they stay only for a moment, other times they linger for much longer, eating away at us until we are nervous wrecks. That's how it is for me, anyway, though one can only ever know their own thoughts. I was once told that I'd be surprised at how many people feel this way inside, though right now I beg to differ. Nobody could be feeling what I felt; and that's exactly what I've been jotting down in my journal, over and over again.

To my left, I notice a short, Chinese woman, with sleek, black hair, washing her hands in the sink carefully and precisely, as though one wrong move could mess up the whole system she has going on. I sense a little OCD going on with her, but I say nothing, of course; instead, I look over to my right, where a tall, blonde-haired lady, dressed in expensive clothes (a beige coat, with fur around the collar) is checking her appearance. I make a calculated guess that she's Russian from the hard expression she wears, and, of course, her towering height and immaculate beauty; yes, definitely Russian. I wonder if these two women I currently share my surroundings with have made any assumptions about me; I wonder which flight they will be on, and whether they are going home, on vacation, or travelling on urgent business overseas. Looking into the mirror at my own reflection, I can see that my curly hair is surprisingly tame at the moment – shiny too. My face is a little pale, but that doesn't bother me, because, alongside my bright red lipstick, which I applied moments ago, it gives me that 1940s look, which I like. I love red lipstick, particularly against white skin – I love the harshness of it. The Chinese woman is leaving now; she glances at me just before she turns towards the door. I notice she is about an inch smaller than I am, as opposed to the Russian lady, who is perhaps double my height. Now she is leaving too. I have always focused on those around me; I'm a people-watcher. I'm quiet in the company of others – large groups in particular – but I'm always observing, always watching, always thinking.

Who puts these *thoughts* into our heads?

What is my purpose here, now, stood in this bathroom, washing my hands?

Why are bathrooms almost always painted white?

11

If I had just one wish, right at this very moment, I'd wish I could do something about *my thoughts*. Maybe suppressing them would be the most desirable choice, because, right now, they overpower me; they take over my entire mind and body; they present themselves through a series of vivid flashbacks, so lifelike and real that I no longer know past from present. I know for sure that something isn't quite right with me, and if I could find the root of this, then maybe I would be okay. Maybe I could live a happy, normal life, in a red-brick house, surrounded by a garden of white, yellow, and pink roses and a white picket fence. I would like red roses too, just in front of the door (which would be white) – a subtle and stylish touch, like red lipstick against white skin.

The little details have always been of great importance to me; it's the same in life, for it's often the little things that take up the biggest spaces in our hearts: warm hugs, good manners, friendly smiles, and kind gestures. It doesn't matter how big or well-decorated our homes are, nor the amount of money in the bank. The job is not that much more important either, because, at the end of the day, these material things can disappear in an instant; one wrong move, and they can come crashing down, just like the Twin Towers on the eleventh day of September. But the *feeling* that is planted inside us through a small gesture of kindness – a warm smile or a hug; that feeling will always remain there, and might well have a significant impact on our next move through the journey of life. Take the Twin Towers, for instance; we don't hear stories about the occupations of the individuals that lost their lives, nor the amount of money they had, *but the lives themselves*: the loved ones, and the messages they left behind, those last phone calls, wives left without husbands, and children left without parents. It was the emotion, the love, the loss

– that's what was spoken about, and still is to this very day. It is those things that will, in a sense, go on *living,* in our hearts and our minds, forever.

Isn't that beautiful? That despite the tragedy, the deaths, the brutality of the actions that day, love still conquers all, and creates an eternal life through memories and stories that will continue to be told, generation after generation after generation.

I have lost a lot. And then, there are some things I never even had to begin with. But, despite the loss, neglect, betrayal, and heartache, I *do* remember her tight hugs, the way she made me laugh at random moments, day and night, and, most of all, the adventures we shared. I cling on to those memories so tightly, replaying them every day, trying to make them clearer and clearer. It's as though I'm painting a picture, gradually adding more detail until it is the image that once existed. Sometimes, these images become tarnished by the more tragic and darker scenes that occurred, but this doesn't seem to be within my control just now.

The cold water feels refreshing against the warm clamminess of my hands. I am in the bathroom, in London Heathrow Airport, washing away the white soap suds that came from the white dispenser fixated to a white wall; I will travel soon. A whirlwind of thoughts, ideas, and dreams consume me. A-hundred-and-one possible scenarios enter my mind without my consent, though, through careful, calculated analysing and planning, I hope that I can somehow be prepared for everything that is to come. The announcement for the next flight to Hong Kong echoes loudly, filling the atmosphere; it's telling people that the boarding gate has now opened, though this is not my flight. Perhaps the Chinese woman who was here just a moment ago will take this flight. But me? I can

13

stay here a moment longer. I return to the cubicle – the same one I just left. I close the door, and sit to resume a little light reading, crossing my legs and uncrossing them again, trying to get comfortable on this harsh floor, which was never intended for such a purpose. The bathroom floor in Heathrow Airport is not the cleanliest, or most ideal, place to sit, but it provides the isolation that I need. I feel I really need the privacy, to shut myself off if only for a few minutes; that, and the security of the walls and confined space. I feel it is only the strength and sturdiness of these walls that is holding me up right now. There won't be much time for that later – the privacy, I mean. So here I sit, with my back propped up against the wall and my knees pulled close to my chest, like a tiny hedgehog protecting itself. I am protecting myself, though from what exactly I am unsure. I'm resting my leather-bound journal on top of my knees, holding it open with the tips of my fingers, scanning and digesting the words, whilst searching for last minute answers.

A while ago now, I began keeping this diary/journal of my daily thoughts, feelings, worries, and anxieties. I began to write things down because it was the advice of my psychiatrist, and also because this last year has been a rather interesting and eventful period in my life – a highly destructive and negative one, unfortunately, but, all the same, a time that I agreed needed documenting. I love writing – I can't express just how much, but I do really love to put pen to paper – so naturally a diary seemed a good idea. Healthy too, or so I'd heard. And later, there is always the possibility to look back at those thoughts that are presented so clearly, and analyse them with new eyes. When I write, I feel I can communicate anything I desire or need, and it all stays between me, my pen, and the paper I write upon. This is ideal, for my sense of trust has been tried and tested to the extreme over the years. Writing is something personal, delicate, and soothing; I can do it in the morning sat on my bed, while I eat in the kitchen, or even sitting on the bathroom floor in Heathrow Airport. My paper and pen have never judged me, or made me feel uncomfortable; for this reason, I trust them. We all need to direct our thoughts somewhere – mostly towards friends and family. Yet, some of us – the lonely and isolated ones – must find alternatives. And so it is that I make do with a single pen, and an unlimited amount of paper.

It's quite cold now, even in the airport beneath my white, woolly jumper and scarf, though soon, when I travel, I will be heading somewhere much warmer. So, for now, I am happy to be surrounded by that coolness, just writing, and enjoying that beautiful freedom it offers me. Another reason I have come to favour the 'keeping a diary' idea is perhaps the most important one of all; I believe it will be the thing I leave behind of myself, my mark, that will hopefully remain – you know, after I'm gone.

Chapter Two

Three months earlier… London, February 2015

I was so scared it hurt. I felt sick constantly. I wanted to die.

Have you ever really, well and truly, hated yourself, to the point of being utterly disgusted and ashamed by your very existence?

I have.

Some days, I hated myself so much that I tore away at my flesh, in the hope that there would be something more beautiful beneath it. I really, well and truly, hated myself. I hated having this *wretched*, *decrepit*, *psychotic* character, that made me so unlike any of those around me. I was *abnormal* – an *outcast* – and I just couldn't accept it anymore. Mostly, it was the fear that caused me to unravel – a dark fear that consumed me. Yet, nobody understood: my friends didn't understand, my sister didn't understand – *I* didn't even understand. It was pure torture in its rawest form, and I was so tired of trying to be understood – trying to explain myself to people, whilst, with tears in my eyes and frustration in my heart, I swallowed their shallow advice about going for a walk, taking a holiday, or, my favourite, 'reading a book'. No; nobody understood. They would never have filled my ears with such absurd suggestions if they'd known how I really felt.

Voices from the past invaded the present, poisoning it beyond recognition, and destroying any possibility of new friendships, or hope of a normal future. I was lonely all the time, so incredibly lonely, and all I wanted was to be held. But how, when I was unable to form connections anymore? Those days were long gone. However dramatic all of this sounds, it was *exactly* how I felt, not just today, but most days, and though words didn't seem to be enough to describe these feelings, the marks across my arms, my wrists, and my stomach, to some extent *did* illustrate them.

Was it normal to be this scared all the time?

No, it wasn't normal – I knew this – and that's why I didn't tell people I was so afraid.

I didn't tell them I was scared when the telephone rang, when I heard a knock at the door, or when that high-pitched door-bell still echoed at the back of my mind. No; this I kept to myself. I was scared. I was scared because I didn't know what I was doing; I didn't know who I was, or what I was waiting for, and, for now, I had no choice but to live inside this fiery circle of infinite loneliness and confusion, constantly being burned by its ravenous flames. Those flames were *real*; they were red-hot, burning flames, and they ate away at me every day, but most of all at night. With the night came the greatest fear – a feeling of dread, accompanied by a sickening sensation in the pit of my stomach. I hated the night times.

Had I lost control of my emotions?

Was I powerless to regain my own well-being?

Would I make it to the age of thirty?

Like everybody, I had a past, yet my story was a very complicated and obscure one, like one of Francis Bacon's paintings: raw, grotesque, and frightening. It was a story I couldn't fully make sense of – not alone anyway. I required some assistance to put all of the pieces together, and understand why I was so afraid all the time, because it was becoming more apparent each day that this pain that existed inside of me – this fear and dread; it wasn't right. Imagine, just for one moment, that you are being impaled by a thousand sharpened knives, over and over again, but never being fortunate enough to die from their harsh wounds. You know that, each time the next set of knives is thrust into your flesh, the pain will be exactly the same, if not worse. But you won't die; you will just keep on reliving the pain. That's what it was like living inside my head. Do you think I'm being over-dramatic when I say I wanted to die, right there, right then, just so it would all end?

I'm not being dramatic; this was how I felt. I felt *desperate*.

Have I expressed myself yet?
Does anybody understand?
STOP.
FINISH.
GO.
LEAVE.
CRY.
HURT.
PAIN.
STAB.
BLOOD.
CUT.

Terrible things had happened to me – painful, twisted, unforeseeable events and situations, which still formed horrific images in my mind. Each one had been a potential trigger to my loss of control, though the final event, I knew, was the real reason for my mental breakdown – for my constant, ongoing pain and self-destruction. These 'things' were always present, always haunting me at the back of every thought and action; these infectious images from the past remained, and I couldn't control them; I couldn't push them aside; in fact, I felt *they* were pushing *me* aside.

Why couldn't I just feel safe? What would it take to go to sleep at night and feel warmth and security?

I hadn't felt safe for a long time now, and I felt so disconnected from myself, and all those around me. It was like, through distorted lenses, I was watching everyone go on living, whilst I, on the other hand, remained frozen in this vicious cycle of self-destruction. I was frozen within a specific moment in time, and it was hurting me so much.

I needed help.

My name is Abi – short for Abigail – though I have never favoured the name, hence my shortening it to Abi. I'm twenty-seven years old, and *sometimes* I live with my sister, when I'm not travelling from country to country, trying to hold down a job in a hotel, or on a holiday resort. I love to travel to different countries, see new sights, and meet new people; it's always kind of been 'my thing'. So far, I've been to Spain, America, Italy, Belgium, France, Croatia, and Egypt. However, as many new people as I have met, and new friends that I've made on each of these adventures, is the same number that I've managed to lose. An infinite number of reasons, existing deep inside of me, mean that I'm unable to maintain friendships and other relationships; in fact, I am sure that even my sister would have left me had we not shared the same parents. I come and go like a passing breeze. I have always been described as a free spirit; I've been admired by many for my sense of freedom and courage to just leave at any time, but there are cracks in this image that those people do not see – cracks visible only to me. Cracks that run so deep, they have become part of my existence, and the destruction of it.

It was as a result of those cracks that I was here again in England, after a long and tiresome journey; I was here to find out what was wrong with me. Something I was aware of was that, as messed up as I had been before I left, it had been this last venture that had pushed me to the edge. My time in Egypt had been the final blow – the biggest test, and one which I had failed, not making it out without many, many scars. Too much had happened out there. It had been *wrong,* in every sense of the word – *dysfunctional, twisted,* each day another form of *torture* – yet I'd stayed, and I'd let it happen to me. Perhaps I'd been self-harming by doing so, or perhaps I was just holding on to something else.

What was wrong with me?

This question enflamed me, at least five times a day. Five: that was the number of prayers that had echoed from the Mosque each day in Cairo, beckoning the people towards the sound, informing them that it was time to pray. I'd prayed too, when I was there. My friend had taught me how. Dressed in long, flowing robes, and headscarves, we'd prayed together. Sometimes we'd cried afterwards. She used to cry after she had just hurt me, but the praying brought us together again. I used to cry almost every day. In fact, until that period in Cairo, I'd never known it was possible for one person to cry so many tears.

Where did all that water even come from?

Back in London, in the spare room my sister let me reside in, crying into my pillow had become part of my daily routine now. Sometimes, when I cried myself to sleep, I found the next morning that my eyes were so swollen, I looked like I had suffered an allergic reaction to some cosmetic or other, and it took consistent splashing of cold water to banish the evidence, so that I might look acceptable for the day ahead. I hugged my pillow each night, trying to steal any security, love, or affection from it. And then, I remembered it was only a pillow, and objects don't provide the necessities that all humans require. Entering this cruel world as a neglected child had left its scars too, that's for sure, but I hung onto the thought that having a scar was, in fact, a sign of survival. I battled, and the battle was intense. There were many factors combined that had resulted in who I was today. It wasn't just what had happened in Egypt that had messed me up, however I felt like there were pieces missing, and this frustrated me; I didn't feel 'whole' anymore. Actually, I couldn't even remember when this feeling had started, or whether it was something I had always had.

During adolescence, I had often turned towards my teachers in school for support; this I recalled, though, when they'd failed to help me in the way I needed, I'd felt I had no other choice but to turn to the knife, with which I had begun drawing my feelings upon my bare arms, expressing my emotions in such a harsh manner, my flesh tearing with each slash as though it were merely the skin of a ripe peach. I was no peach, though; a bruised prune, perhaps, shrivelled up and confined to the depths of despair.

The first time I had self-harmed, I had been just eleven years old.

When people had noticed the cuts on my arms, it had never been difficult to find other methods of self-destruction. In fact, it was surprising just how many ways there were to hurt one's self: scratching, cutting, biting, burning, depriving one's self of food, binging, vomiting...

I could go on. I had done them all, and my body now told a story of hate, loneliness, loss, anger, and sadness. It sounded so tragic, but I knew that each day I *needed* to, and *would,* secretly sabotage myself, just so I could go on living amongst the rest of the people in a more peaceful state of mind. And, if things got worse, I knew I always had Plan B. Plan B was always lurking at the back of my mind, like a lioness ready to pounce on her significantly weaker prey – I always being the *significantly weaker prey,* of course.

"Are you okay?"

There it was – that familiar, worried voice, seeping in through the crack in the door, bringing me back down to Earth, though it was not the voice I wanted it to be.

It was exactly 9.45 on Tuesday morning. I knew this because, the moment I heard her words, I checked the time on my silver-strapped watch to make sure I wasn't running late. It was okay; I still had another fifteen minutes before we would need to leave. I wiped the damp vomit residue from around my mouth with a piece of tissue paper, before flushing it down, along with the contents of my stomach. My eyes watered implacably, and my throat felt as dry as the Arabian Desert, but now my stomach felt much better. Emptier, which somehow matched my emotions.

"Yes, I'm fine," I replied to Helen, who had by now pushed open the glossy-white bathroom door, and was looking down sorrowfully at her failure of a younger sister. "Sorry," I added, with that same weak, apologetic smile I often used.

I sniffled, and wiped away the water that had formed around my eyes, which I felt sure were once again red and swollen. I was aware of my sister's eyes resting on the

22

blood-stained bandage around my wrist, though I did not care to hide it; she knew what I did, and here she was witnessing yet more of my destructive behaviour. My dignity had shrivelled up and died long ago.

"Oh, Abi…" She shook her head sorrowfully, and reached for a roll of tissue to hand me; "Here."

"Thank you," I said, taking the tissue from her.

I noticed the ceramic tiles below, reflecting our movements in the same way a flowing stream catches the subtle sway of the branches from hovering trees. She was standing there, hovering, with her dark, brown hair neatly swept back, her subtle make-up so carefully applied, and a pair of light, green eyes, watching me with that same look of concern as when we were much younger. I often pitied her for having a messed-up sister like me; I felt guilty, and had desperately tried to fix myself on numerous occasions – if not for myself, then at least for those around me. After all, she'd had a hard time too. Helen was five years older than me, and a much more serious and conscientious individual than I could ever aspire to be. As a child, she had thrown herself into the world of books; she had been a quieter girl than me, barely speaking to anybody, but she'd read incessantly, as though those books held the answers to every piece of knowledge she would need to survive. And, in some ways, I suppose they did, because she was the one who survived. We had shared the same neglect as children; we had been mentally tortured at the hands of our parents, and we had both suffered socially as a result, yet it had affected me differently – *more,* I guess.

Did that make me the weaker one?

I was told, by a past counsellor, that siblings who grow up in the same environment do not always perceive things in the same way; a young girl of, say, five years old, might see a situation completely differently to a girl of, say, fourteen years old, and the impact of these perceptions contributes to their development. That's what she'd said, anyway, and I guess it made some sense to me. I had seen many counsellors and therapists over the years; some had left a pleasant imprint in my heart, whilst there were others whose names I could no longer recall.

I only looked at my sister for a brief moment, and then I retreated to my crouched position, head over the toilet, as though I might be sick again. I wiped my mouth and my nose, and caught another tear as it left my eye, though this time it was not a tear of sadness, but one from the intensity of my earlier vomiting.

"Please, Abi... Enough is enough," said Helen, with a desperation in her voice that I had become familiar with by now.

"Sorry," I replied, almost robotically.

Apologising for my abnormal behaviour had become routine since I'd been back in London, living beneath her roof.

What else could I say?

I was genuinely sorry, yet I felt hopeless and resigned within myself.

She was wearing one of her elegant trouser-suits over a light-blue, fitted blouse, and looked like the graceful woman and high-achiever she was. How I admired her, when I looked down at my own casual style: a white blouse, creased from slouching over the toilet all morning, and a pair of dark, fitted jeans. I guess I could have, on a good day, considered myself stylish – I loved putting together new outfits – but *elegant* was definitely not a word others would use to describe me; I was too clumsy. We couldn't have been more different, my sister and I. One of the differences between us was that she worked at The London College – a prestigious lecturer, teaching

24

English Literature and Language to eighteen-year-olds and above – and she always wore a suit. Me? I hadn't had a job in the past year; I couldn't cope with one. The tiniest bit of pressure seemed to trigger that spiral of chaos I often became trapped in. My sister was much stronger – elegant, quite reserved, and conservative too. I was a free-spirit in every sense of the word: I spoke before I thought, I could be quite bold at times, and I loved to fly off to various countries without warning. And, without warning, I could also fall apart. Yes, we couldn't have been more different, Helen and I.

"I'm working on it, Helen. Just be patient with me, please," I pleaded, earnestly yet unconvincingly.

"I am trying, believe me, but it's not easy to see you like this." She looked away from me, and, for a moment, I thought she was going to walk away.

"You don't have to watch. It's not exactly easy for me either," I said, a little more abruptly than intended. "I've finished now," I added, softening my tone.

"Do you need anything?"

"No, I'm okay. Thank you."

Usually my sister would spend her time preparing lessons for the coming day; she was always busy, always doing something. When she wasn't working, however, she could be found catching up on some leisurely reading, throwing herself into the worlds of Virginia Woolf, James Joyce, and even plays by William Shakespeare. Her taste in literature dated way back to before I was even born, however today, here she was, putting those more civilised characters aside, and helping her wacky, broken sister to stand on her feet once more.

Helen had one hand on the brass door-handle as she turned and looked back at me to speak.

"Okay, well we need to leave in about ten minutes for your appointment with Doctor Green," she said, referring to the psychiatrist who would be talking with me about my self-destructive problems, and the recent events that had led to them.

My sister had sought out Dr. Victoria Green from one of her colleagues at the college where she worked, and was now paying a hefty sum for me to engage in weekly sessions with her. Another thing for me to feel guilty about.

"Okay. What about you? What are your plans for today?" I replied, looking down at the white-tiled flooring, avoiding that uncomfortable eye-contact, as I often did.

"I have a few errands to run, and then I'm at work this afternoon," she said, on her way out of the door, though she stopped reluctantly as I followed this by questions about her work.

"How's your job going? Do you like it?" I asked, offering a diversion from this that I thought she might appreciate.

"It pays the bills. We need to get this sorted, Abi; you can't go on like this," said Helen, shaking her head sorrowfully.

She wasn't interested in my small talk. She was both frustrated and concerned with my behaviour, and had every right to be. She left me sitting on the bathroom floor, with only the bleak, white walls for company.

Like the cutting I had also suffered from bulimia since the age of eleven – a considerably young age to have such an aggressive disorder – though it came and went along with my hurricane of moods. I had met Victoria once already with my sister, for a brief assessment, and she had said they needed to do a further consultation, believing I could really use some additional support in my life from professionals who could understand me. She had suggested I meet with her once a week to begin with, though this might be subject to change to two sessions if necessary. Well, this is what the thin, pouting lady had said to my sister, as I had lost focus part way through the conversation, drifting off into another time and place. Cairo, to be precise, for, in my mind, I had never really left.

I was already dreading going back; it all seemed too serious and structured for my liking. Being in that sanitised, white room, sat before a psychiatrist, made me feel completely stripped bare of all the walls I usually built around myself, and of the fun exterior I so often portrayed to the rest of the world. I just felt like a broken, young girl, who could not find a way to be part of the *normal,* civilised society that continued to exist around her.

"Okay," I said quietly, to myself as much as to my sister.

I looked behind me; I knew she had returned because, in truth, she was just as lost as me; she didn't know what to do with me, or whether it was safe to leave me by myself. She didn't know how to be that caring and affectionate sister, because our parents had robbed her of that ability.

I pitied her, yet I still struggled to make eye contact with her, particularly after what I had just done here in the bathroom – *her* bathroom – and I reviled the fact that she knew about my sickening obsession.

"I'll be ready soon. I just need a moment to…" I spoke so softly that my voice seemed almost a whisper, that eventually disintegrated into the air before my last words could form.

I would pick myself up again, I always did. I just required a little more help this time. I wondered how many other people there were like me, who just didn't fit into the world around them – who had to watch others go on living, whilst they themselves seemed to stroll around the desert in search of water. I wondered, for a moment, if I were perhaps part of a somewhat larger group than I could have imagined. Or was I well and truly alone?

Slowly, and with great effort, for my muscles seemed to have locked, I pushed myself up off the coolness of the tiles, releasing my long, curly hair from the constriction of the metal clip, and then, almost simultaneously, I straightened out the creases on my white, long-sleeved blouse. My face looked different, I noticed. Looking into the oval-shaped mirror above the sink, I could see that, despite my cheeks being a little flushed, I looked much thinner than I had the previous week, and this pleased me. I had green eyes, like my sister's, and they sparkled from the water that had formed around them. My hair was lighter than hers – a light brown, almost blonde – and, for some reason, I had developed this thick mass of curls that nobody else in our family had. I always believed it was to emphasise my wildness. The echo of Helen's light footsteps faded as she went into the living room, whilst I stepped out of the bathroom and into the kitchen, my own high-heeled shoes clicking loudly against the laminate flooring, announcing my catastrophic presence to the world, and leaving behind that weak, sick young woman in the bathroom. My sister and I were both quite short, barely leaving the five-foot mark, so high-heels were a God-send to the both of us. And well, for me, they did add that touch of elegance I lacked in every other area. I inhaled the lemony air-freshener that filled the moderate space, and shuddered as the cool morning air wrapped itself around my slender frame. I could almost feel my bones rattling against each other, alongside the sound of my teeth, which chattered rapidly. I rubbed my hands together, as though they were two sticks that might create a fire if rubbed hard enough. All of my clothes seemed a little looser in these weeks, and made me look poor and pitiful, though even the prospect of a shopping trip could not lift my spirits. Looking around the idealistic scene, and contents within, I admired the way my sister had done up the kitchen, decorating it in bright shades of yellow and iridescent white – happy colours. The only objects I found which were a different colour were the sharp, ruby-red glass fruit bowl, and its glittering contents: two shiny red apples, a bunch of purple grapes that shone like small jewels, and three ripe bananas still attached by the stem. However, no food could evoke my appetite this morning; my overwhelming anxiety, and the sickening sensation in the pit of my stomach, seemed like a meal in themselves. Standing by the window, with the palms of my hands resting on the newly furnished worktop, I gazed out of the double-glazing at the busy, grey road below, imagining the smell of fumes entering my nose from the cars. I imagined the cool breeze blowing on my skin, sending my curls into a wild dance around my face, and I smiled at the prospect of this, as though I had somehow brought my thoughts to life. I loved London, and had missed it immensely while I'd been away; I enjoyed its energy, and, living in the centre, we got to see a lot of it. But still, all I could think about at that moment, as I looked down on those grey streets, was Egypt, and my friend I had left behind.

A moment passed by, though I had no idea how long it had been, or what I had been doing; suddenly, the time had moved forward without me, and it was time to head on out to that much-anticipated meeting.

"Let's go!" came my sister's voice from the top of the stairs, as she fiddled in her beige Jimmy Choo handbag for her keys. "We should try to at least make a good impression by arriving on time, don't you think?"

It was a rhetorical question, meaning I wasn't obliged to answer, just obey. I was used to that – being led places, and told what I should and should not do. My time in Egypt had been very much that way, with me being quite dependent on another, as well as under the constant watch of a third, and less-appreciated, presence.

My sister's bag was always overflowing with the items she required for her busy lifestyle. My own bag – a small, black, leather shoulder bag – contained only my phone and my purse, though today I had no use for either of them.

"I don't think the purpose of me seeing a psychiatrist is to make a good impression," I said, rolling my eyes, unable to bite my tongue.

Despite my brief wave of positivity earlier in the kitchen, my mood was now foul at the very prospect of seeing a psychiatrist, and I felt the need to demonstrate this at every given moment. I was angry again, yet this was mixed with anxiety and fear; I could feel that familiar tensing of my stomach muscles, and the dryness in my mouth.

"Abi!"

"I'm just saying… it's probably better she sees me at my worst."

"Promise me you'll take this seriously today." She looked at me with that solemn expression I had seen many times; it was starting to irritate me just a little, for little did she know, it hurt.

30

My sister's voice wasn't exactly sympathetic or nurturing; in fact, she appeared to be more frustrated than usual today, which I felt solely responsible for, as I silently swallowed the pain her harsh tone caused me.

"I'm ready," I replied reluctantly, with an air of frustration in my own voice.

"Okay, let's go."

I edged closer, slowly, in response to my sister's words, yet without much feeling, stepping on those dark swirls on the maroon-carpeted stairs, balancing in my high shoes as I walked down them, out of the door, and into the hustle and bustle of that long, grey street. I was grateful for the black, knee-length coat my sister had given me to wear, for the weather was much colder than what I had been living with for the past year. My sister was used to it, and had a wardrobe full of winter-wonders. She was wearing an elegant, beige coat, which matched her handbag. We walked a whole ten minutes without uttering a single word, or even making a glance at one another, as the cars sped past left, right, and centre, leaving behind thick trails of smoke from their noisy engines. I was thankful that it was this way; I didn't feel much like speaking. In fact, if I'd had the option that morning to curl into a ball, and remain beneath a large rock, I would have. In the height of my anxiety, I didn't feel the freshness of the breeze on my face that I had imagined in the kitchen, nor did I respond to the sound of all that traffic buzzing past me, inches from my body, as we crossed the road. Even the birds in the trees failed to capture my attention. Everything was silent, right up until I entered that small, white room, and sat down on that blue-cushioned chair across from her. Everything was a blur, a haze, a dark dream.

Another moment passed on by without my consent, and, as I tried desperately to catch up, I found myself already sat across from her: Dr. Victoria Green, with a set of large, brown eyes, analysing me right from the start.

"How are you today, Abi?" she asked me, in a monotone voice, not used for friends or family, but more likely for hospital patients, customers in a shop, or even a telephone answering-machine; yes, her voice would have been perfect for any one of those scenarios. "Is it okay if I call you Abi, or do you prefer Abigail?"

"Abi is fine," I responded in an equally senseless voice. "Thanks," I added, rolling my eyes, but then instantly regretted it, as I saw she was still looking at me, fixated on my cold gaze.

'Not a good start,' I thought to myself, as my sister's words about taking this seriously echoed in the back of my mind.

She turned towards her laptop and typed something simultaneously to my response. I imagined she was writing something along the lines of: *Patient shows signs of hostility and anger*. If she'd written that, then she would have been correct; I *was* feeling rather hostile, and a touch angry too. I felt inferior and abnormal sitting before her – something I did not need more of in my life – so I turned my attention to my surroundings, in hope that they would help me relax. On the small, wooden table, which was the only thing that separated me from her, was a glass vase about fifteen inches tall. It was filled half-way with water, and contained a bouquet of chrysanthemums in yellow, white, and orange. They added an air of positivity to the atmosphere, so much so that they caused me to smile for the first time that morning. Sitting back on the chair, I allowed the softness of it to ingest me, ever so slightly, until I not only felt relaxed, but most likely appeared relaxed too.

"The weather is nice outside today, don't you think?" said Victoria, as though trying again to engage with me, a little more humane this time, though still not what I would call friendly.

"Yes," I replied, with a nod and a light smile. "A little cold, but bearable I guess."

The cold had been really hard during my first few days here, especially when I had stepped off the plane in sandals and a t-shirt during a harsh blizzard, though now it was getting a little easier to cope with.

"You will have to bear with me while I fill out a few forms, okay Abi? It's just standard procedure, and it shouldn't take too long."

"Okay. No problem."

"Do you like the flowers?" she asked me, and I realised then that she must have been observing me whilst I had been admiring them just moments ago.

"Yes, they're beautiful," I replied, glancing over at them again.

I wondered if she had seen me smile at them earlier.

About four feet above the table bearing the flowers was a small painting, featuring a green meadow, cut down the centre by a thin, blue stream that ran this way and that like the veins upon my arms. This, too, had an air of positivity about it.

Dr. Green typed away on the sleek, black computer that was propped open on her desk; she swivelled around several times as she did so on her black, leather chair, asking me questions to confirm my identity and past medical history. It seemed to go on like this for an entire hour, though, when I looked down at my watch, I saw that only six minutes had passed. I tried my best to look obliging, and be polite with her from the beginning, though I must admit it was a challenge, as I had started to get myself worked up again. I got through it only by taking slow, deep breaths – in for the count of four, out for the count of seven – and reassuring myself it would all be over soon.

"Okay then, let's get started," she said, turning to face me, studying me first from head to toe, before offering me a light, sympathetic smile. "How are you feeling just now?"

"Nervous," I replied, in a voice that portrayed every ounce of it; my frustration had subsided during those six minutes, and had been replaced with a growing anxiety at the prospect of all the personal questions I knew were yet to come.

"That's perfectly understandable," she said, with a gentle smile. "But you can relax here. I want this to become a place you can feel comfortable in, and share your thoughts, feelings, and anxieties."

I let out a nervous laugh, and responded with the words: "I don't really feel comfortable anywhere, or with anyone, Dr. Green."

"Well, first of all, you can call me Victoria," she said with a smile.

Victoria looked across at me thoughtfully, and I wondered what she was thinking – what assumptions she was making about me, and what question she was about to ask me next.

"To begin with, Abi, I wondered if you could tell me why you think your sister brought you here to see me?" she asked calmly.

I looked down at the laminate flooring beneath my feet, and thought for a moment about the events earlier this morning – the scene in the bathroom, and my sister looming over me. Sadness consumed me, mixed with humiliation, and a loneliness, which may have actually been the strongest emotion I was feeling, though I couldn't be sure.

"Well, it's because I'm self-harming. I do this in various ways... and I... I just struggle, I guess. My emotions, thoughts, and feelings aren't normal."

The polished flooring caught my gaze again, for I was already feeling embarrassed of myself and the words coming from my mouth.

"Okay. Why don't you think they are normal, Abi?"

"It's the intensity of them, I guess, and the result being that I cannot handle that intensity, so I self-harm... or act irrationally... impulsively... I just make a lot of mistakes. I feel that... there aren't any words big enough to describe how I feel. So I cut myself. And somehow this expresses what's going on inside." I stopped, for the pace of my breathing had quickened, and I struggled to get some of my words out. "I don't know if that makes any sense?" I added, "but that's how it is for me."

"Don't worry, you explained to me very well, and that does make sense. People who self-harm often describe it in a similar way to how you have just described it."

"Oh. Okay."

I inhaled and exhaled deeply, in an attempt to steady my nerves.

"The first step in therapy is to acknowledge that there is an issue, and I can see that you are doing that, so this is a very good start, Abi."

A shy smile crept across my face, involuntarily, for the flattery and being praised for something, even though it was so minor, just felt warm, and made my body feel all tingly. This embarrassed me, and I quickly turned my expression to a serious one.

35

"What do you hope to get from these sessions?" she asked me, tilting her head ever so slightly to the left.

"I just want to be normal... to be able to cope with situations more effectively, without the self-harm. I want to be able to have normal friendships, without my strange behaviour corrupting everything. I don't want to be humiliated anymore."

"Hmm, that seems a fair assessment. Well, to begin with, Abi, I wondered if you could outline to me your relationships with other people: friends, family, boyfriends, *girlfriends*. Would you say you have been in some *intense* relationships within the past year?"

My eyes studied Victoria Green, whilst I considered how to begin to answer such a big question. Analysing the details of her face, her outfit, and even the way she sat, so perfectly poised, I tried to plant these attributes in my memory, in case they might serve a purpose later on. The thing I understood about being in therapy was that I wasn't obliged to ask her questions about herself, nor would she offer any personal information if she did her job correctly, so I needed to make my own observations, and that's what I was doing as I lost myself in thought. Meanwhile, I saw that she was studying me. 'How ironic', I thought to myself.

I liked the fitted, black suit-jacket she was wearing; it appeared to be tailor-made, clinging to her slim frame, and the black trousers too, which were made from an expensive, shimmery material. My eyes discreetly looked down at her suede boots; they were very elegant too – high-heeled – and were the perfect accompaniment to her outfit. From this, I understood she must have received a good salary, as well as having an eye for detail – a gift for putting outfits together. Perhaps my sister would have had more luck than me engaging with this woman, *this lady*;

they could have drank Chardonnay together, and talked about how elegant and perfect they both were.

"Abi!"

"Yes?"

Her voice startled me away from those careful observations, leaving me with the sense of having an unfinished task which now hung over me, as the sound of my name still echoed. My mind floated softly back into the small, white room, and, for the briefest of moments, it was as though I had been slowly landing a parachute, losing myself in a simple, mountain view. And then I had fallen, right upon hearing my name being called. I glared at her more harshly than intended. I don't know why, but I had a slight wave of anger towards her just then; she hadn't done anything wrong, but I suddenly felt I *needed* to dislike her. It would be less painful that way, rather than getting attached to somebody again. I realised she was still waiting for my response. Gathering my thoughts, I tried desperately to cast aside any other opinions, judgements, and observations that kept trying to enter without my consent, and, eventually, I did manage to turn my focus towards our meeting – one which I now hoped would come to an end soon.

"Sorry, what was the question?" I asked, feeling shameful at having been so far away, and not possessing any memory as to what had been asked.

"Your past relationships; would you describe them as being intense?"

"Ah… yes… sorry, I just… Yes, I guess I could describe some of my past relationships as intense," I replied, finally beginning to focus once again.

My voice came out rather scrambled and high-pitched in comparison to Victoria Green's, who spoke in such an articulate, polite, and demure manner. It was easy to see she was educated, not just from her voice, but from her appearance, which I had so carefully analysed several times now. Her dark-brown hair was sleek and straight like my sister's, and her make-up as subtle and carefully applied as any woman in such a high profession. Everything about her seemed expensive and well-calculated, as though she had woken up two hours early to put it all together – every shade, tone, and colour. Despite having being in her presence for less than thirty minutes, I knew she was a serious woman, and I felt this the entire time we were in that small room, where the white walls kept moving in on me. White – the colour of medicine and doctors.

However, I had to admit, Victoria did possess some beauty, and normally I liked speaking to beautiful women, for I had always felt that surely, if they were that beautiful on the outside, then there had to be something beautiful on the inside too. That's how I viewed it, anyway, though it wasn't always true. After a moment's reconciliation, while she watched me and I watched her, I decided that I would work with her, and give her the chance that I gave to all women who held some outer beauty. Though, to be completely honest, I didn't even know how to begin to answer some of the questions she presented me with. Each one seemed so deep-rooted that they required careful consideration before speaking, and my mind was anything but clear. Nonetheless, the clock ticked, and somehow, within the following thirty minutes, I managed to describe to her some element of what had happened in Cairo, and also the *intensity* of my relationships whilst I was there. Whether or not this made any sense to her, I wasn't sure, for I presented her with such a stuttered and jumbled recollection of all those events, it must have sounded quite confusing. All the while I spoke, I didn't dare make eye-contact, though I was constantly wary of her looking at me, observing me, analysing my every move, which was quite distracting, and made me even more nervous. Yet still I spoke, because I felt I had no choice, presenting her with a vast haze of words in a muddled order, leaving her with the task of unscrambling them. I spoke and I spoke until I was tired and needed to take those deep breaths again: in for four, and out for seven. I checked her expression, and saw that it had remained the same, giving me no indication as to what it was she thought of me, or what she kept typing on her laptop, simultaneous with every sentence I delivered. This made me feel very uneasy.

"Would you describe yourself as anxious?" she asked, as though reading the next question on her list.

"Right now, or in general?" I asked, smiling awkwardly, as though the answers would be different.

"In general." Victoria smiled back at me, gently, and two tiny cracks appeared on her skin, which had appeared flawless just moments ago.

"Yes, I do feel quite anxious sometimes," I replied, taking a long, deep breath, which perhaps emphasised just how anxious I was feeling, even within this very moment. "I'm not so anxious with the people I trust and feel close with, but everybody else, yes; I'm very anxious, and find it difficult to trust and speak with them."

"And right now?"

"Yes."

"Why do you think that is?" she said softly.

I thought for a moment.

"I guess... because I feel I am being analysed."

"Do you think I am judging you?"

I hesitated. "A little."

"I will never judge you. I am here to listen, help you make sense of things. But I will never, ever judge you." She smiled again.

"I can't help but notice you have an accent – not a British accent. Were you born in the UK, or…?"

I smiled.

"I know, I know; everybody comments on this." It was true, my accent was completely off, and it had been like that for some time now. "I guess it's just from travelling a lot."

She typed something into her computer.

'Oh, great, what now?' I thought to myself, as though I had just unknowingly produced another symptom for something or other.

I frowned, nervously pulling at the hem of my white blouse, trying to straighten it of all the creases. When I let go, they returned. This session seemed to be going on forever, though I didn't dare look at my watch again. After a series of yet more personal and in-depth questions, which had required a lot of thinking on my part, I was fully engaged with her now, as she asked me the next question, and it began to slowly feel like we were at least on the same level, and not just in the same room.

"Okay," she said, and once again typed something on her laptop; "do you feel that other people are judging you, Abi?"

Continuing to breathe deeply, I felt tears lurking in the distance, though thankfully I was able to swallow them.

"Yes, I do," I said quietly. "Though since I returned to England, I haven't met too many people, as I have found it difficult to communicate with anybody… or trust… I just… I prefer to be left alone now. I feel… I feel that… I cannot connect… with *anybody,* and I'm just not okay anymore." I spoke with hand gestures, as I began to stutter

40

even more, and felt my words were not enough to describe what I felt.

I looked at her, and she nodded her head. There were times that I felt I wasn't even British anymore, particularly when I struggled to find the right words in English.

"It's okay that you feel like that. Do you have anybody here that you are close with?

"No."

"But you were close with your friends in Egypt, am I right?"

"Yes."

"Hmm." She muttered something quietly to herself that I couldn't hear; "Well, this is something we will explore together in these sessions. I'm sorry about all the questions today, but I need to get a clear picture of what exactly is going on with you, so we can provide the right help."

"It's okay," I replied, with a light smile.

Some of her questions did feel quite heavy to bear, and they certainly weren't helping the *anxiety*. However, she had just apologised, and I was clinging hopefully onto this further sign of humanity from her.

"Well, Abi, as you know, your sister and I have spoken about you, and she is concerned for your mental health and wellbeing. So, based upon the information I have already, I think that, over the next few sessions, I would like to focus on your relationships with *people*, and your relationship, not just with others, but also with yourself," she said, turning away from her laptop and looking me straight in the eye.

"Okay," I said, feeling slightly hostile and nervous again.

I couldn't help but feel that the way she put the stress on the word 'people' seemed to be done in a provocative manner, and it bothered me profusely. I didn't know exactly why, but it made me feel somewhat alien, living in a world full of normal citizens; it felt like she was insinuating already that I was not part of this group. Yes, I already knew I was a bit of an outsider, and understood that I probably didn't fit in as well as I should, but having somebody else state it so boldly made me feel all the more aware of how different I was. And I did not welcome these words.

"Okay," I repeated, unsure of what would be next to spill from her tongue, and what my relationships had to do with my bulimia; after all, that was supposedly why I was here – because I over-ate and made myself sick.

My moods seemed to switch quite rapidly during the session with Victoria; one moment I felt she was soft, calm, and empathising with me, and the next it seemed like she was attacking me. Yet, *was* it her, or was it my messed-up way of perceiving things?

"I am aware you have been living with a man and woman in Egypt for some time, is that correct?" asked Victoria.

She began inspecting me a little more closely, as though the answer might be written across my forehead, or in my green eyes, which I held in a strong glare, as though I was giving her some of my anger. Maybe she couldn't even get her head around the concept, and needed to look me in the eyes to find the truth. Whatever the reason, I didn't like the eye-contact.

"Yes. That's correct," I said, in a tone that portrayed a clear feeling of hostility, which I felt sure Victoria noticed, for she stared at me a moment longer. And I realised then that I *wanted* her to notice.

42

I wanted her to see my anger. Suddenly, I wanted that confrontation, and an excuse to release some of my pain. I felt my eyes water a little, though I could not pinpoint the exact reason as to why. I wished Leila were here. I missed her immensely, especially now, right at this moment. Taking a deep breath, in for four, and out for seven, I looked at Victoria without even a hint of a smile or kindness in my eyes. She looked back at me with a delicate empathy, which evoked even more awkwardness and anger from me.

Why was she doing this?

Why was she toying with my emotions?

She rubbed her chin thoughtfully, tilting her head ever so slightly to the left, which seemed to be a habit of hers. She smiled sympathetically.

"It's okay to be upset, angry, confused. I will help you understand it, and work through these emotions."

I nodded my head, glancing over at the vase of flowers and hoping that I might absorb some more of their positivity, as I had done earlier.

"I just miss my friends in Egypt. We lived together, the three of us, for a long time. It wasn't a healthy relationship between us, but I miss them."

There was a pause, a moment where we seemed to communicate just through our eyes; mine, which were filled with tears and sadness, and hers, which portrayed both empathy and understanding, though it seemed to get lost in her next question.

"Was this relationship between the three of you sexual?" Victoria asked me, quietly, yet completely out of the blue.

Her expression remained the same – empathetic, understanding, and non-judgemental – though mine quickly changed to one of surprise. I was surprised at being confronted so bluntly about a subject so personal, and of an intimate nature.

"What?" I blurted out. "What relevance does this have?" I said, immediately becoming defensive and agitated.

I sensed then that she wanted me to react; perhaps she was intrigued by my anger, enjoying it even. The alarm bells began to ring out inside of me, quiet at first, though they grew louder and louder like the siren on a police car. This was only the first session, and Victoria Green was already crossing into forbidden territory – a territory she had no right to explore, nor did I permit her to enter. I was on the verge of getting up and walking out of the room, but I didn't; I remained seated.

"Why… why are you asking me that?" I stammered, quite possibly shaking at the same time, though I did not know.

"Do you not feel like you can answer that question just now?" she asked softly.

"I… I don't know."

Not only was I upset; I felt completely humiliated, for, despite having lead quite an 'abnormal' lifestyle, I was still incredibly reserved when it came to talking about any intimate details of my past, especially with strangers. And, let's face it, Victoria Green was a stranger. She hadn't even made the effort to get to know me; no, she'd just jumped right on in, and put her feet up on the couch. I felt my cheeks start to burn into that familiar crimson – the same colour as the paint on my sister's living-room walls – and how I longed to open a window and hang my head out of it. In fact, perhaps in that moment, jumping from it would have been the favourable option. I knew she could see my discomfort; I knew she could see the redness in my cheeks, and I felt weakened and inferior, – so much so that I wanted to cry and throw a tantrum, scream, hit the wall. But I didn't. I didn't, because I knew, when I was in the privacy of my own room, I could release my anger and discomfort in my own way, without anyone's knowledge.

"I'm sorry that my question upsets you. Perhaps you could start by telling me why it is such a painful subject?"

Chapter Three

Cairo, December 2014

"YES! It's true! I fucking hate Mohamed!"

My breathing had become heavy and unstable, my face red and swollen, stained with tears as I spat out the words that had been locked up inside of me for so long. I rarely used such strong language, but that just went to show how angry I really was, deep inside the core of my stomach; it was all coming to the surface. Leila looked at me with a sudden shock in her eyes, her jaw almost touching the ground, for I had never before had the courage to scream out these words so clearly at her. Tear upon tear ran down my face, for it wasn't just anger I felt – it was hurt and sadness. There was a growing pain in my head and heart that was so intense I thought that alone would be the cause of my death that night.

"WHAT DO YOU WANT ME TO DO? YOU WANT ME TO LEAVE HIM?" she screamed back at me, hitting both her hands hard on the wall beside her like a woman possessed.

Leila screamed loudly, still hitting the wall, which was already stained by the marks from previous owners. Everything within those walls seemed old, used, dirty, and broken. I felt my feet frozen to the grey-white tiled floor below, though the rest of my body was shaking uncontrollably. Now she was using her fists, banging them harder and harder against the wall behind the television, whilst I just stood there, watching her, feeling so sad at what we had become, yet at the same time, afraid – afraid of how this fight was going to end. Even though, at that moment, the room was filled with screaming, shouting, and cups being shattered as they hit the wall, all had gone silent inside my own head. It was as though the intensity of it all was just too much.

I'd met Leila when I was backpacking across the Middle East, in the heat of June 2013, not so long ago. It was the aftermath of the Egyptian revolution, and Cairo was still filled with street brawls and violent protests, yet strangely it was also mixed with parties and celebrations, where large crowds would wave flags: red, white, and black – those were Egypt's colours. Tahrir Square was always the hotspot for much of Cairo's action, and where all the crowds would form, surrounded by soldiers sat on large tanks, guns at the ready. And it was just a brief walk away from there that I'd met her. I was just standing there, on El Tahrir Bridge, admiring the view of the majestic Nile, which holds so much history and value to the Egyptians, when I saw a young woman with a slender figure, dark-brown hair fastened back with a silver clip, and the most exquisite, chiselled cheek-bones I had ever seen. Two bright-green eyes, just like my own, glistening beneath Egypt's ever-present sun, looked back at me that day as I spoke to her, unknowing of the implications she was to have on my future.

"Excuse me, would you mind taking a photograph of me by the Nile?" I had asked her, motioning to my camera.

I spoke slowly, just in case she didn't speak any English, as I had quickly discovered not many Egyptians in Cairo did. She turned to face me, and a delicate, thoughtful smile appeared on her face, as though a small light had suddenly been switched on inside of her.

"Yes, of course," she replied immediately, carefully taking my camera in her hands as I showed her what to press, before taking position on the bridge.

Good, she did speak English, and, as it turned out, she was a good photographer too, taking three or four pictures for me so that I might choose the ones I liked the most. Not everybody would have done that; sometimes when I asked somebody to take a photo, I got one hideous looking one, or it didn't even develop. But I liked all of the photos that she took of me.

"Thank you, thank you so much," I replied, with a sincere smile, and a voice filled with an unexpected energy – an energy that sprouted from the beautiful scene surrounding us. There's something about being by the water that has always made me feel much more *alive* than anywhere else.

One of the peculiar things about Cairo is that everything seems to be the colour of sand; the buildings, the roads, the street dogs, and even the children, whose clothes, once colourful and clean, now bear that same sandy colour. I was told that, because it hardly ever rains in Egypt, the dust is never washed away from its streets, or the crumbling buildings that tower above, and that's why everything is this worn, sandy colour. Except for the Nile, that is. That day, the Nile was a sparkling reflection of the sky – a glittering blue, mixed with a shimmer of sunlight, and a dash of green, here and there, from the plants that grew on the river banks. A large ship called Nile City rested on the water's surface, offering fine dining for those rare few that could pay the hefty sum to enter. Most of Cairo's top hotels were located by the river, so it was perhaps the place with the most money looming. It was imaginably the most beautiful place in all of Cairo for a friendship to begin, and the sense of possibility that lingered in the air drew me right on in, like a fish lured by bait.

Just as I was about to walk away, she stopped me and asked me my name. She was very sweet, and, though her English was a little broken in some areas, as we slowly got to know each other, I promised her I would help her improve this.

"My name is Abi," I told her; "What's yours?"

"Leila," she responded, still smiling.

A young Egyptian boy walked past us, selling bread from the bakery to anyone who would buy it: just one Egyptian pound, equivalent to approximately ten pence. He carried it on a large stick, all the rings piled on top of each other.

"AISH B'GUINEA!" he called, as he continued across the bridge.

Leila smiled, and asked me if I wanted to try it, but I shook my head, telling her that this kind of bread was something we had a lot of in England, though I loved traditional Egyptian bread, which was flat and round.

I often look back on that day, and wonder how my life would have turned out had I asked somebody else to take that photograph of me. Would Leila and I still have met, maybe in some other area of Cairo, on another day?

I do not know, but I am glad, to some extent, that she was the one standing there. Even now, I can still smell the freshness of the air surrounding the Nile, and hear the sound of the water's natural song as the light breeze hits the surface, creating those high notes unique only to the river. I remember how I liked to lose myself in the glittering reflection of sunlight into water; I could engage in a silent conversation with it for hours on end and never grow tired of its company. On occasions, I would sit outside the Hilton Hotel, not too far away from the water, and watch in awe as the rich Saudi families went in and out. The women always fascinated me the most, with their long black robes, thick eye-liner as black as night, and the way they were always dowsed in expensive perfume and jewels, bought for them by their husbands. It was Leila who had first pointed this out to me and, afterwards, I could always pick out the Arabs from all the other nationalities that would walk on by.

I liked her, Leila, from quite early on, and then somehow, in the mist of it all, I grew to love her. But, after some time, when *we* – the three of us that is – had all been tried and tested, stretched and twisted, prodded and poked, Leila had pushed me to the extreme. And, to this day, I don't know if she feels any remorse about the pain she put me through, or the implications she had on my well-being. But I do know that, underneath all that anger, all those hurtful remarks, and all that selfishness, *she loved me back*.

"I DON'T LOVE HIM! I just want to stay with you! Why can't you understand that, all along, that's all I ever wanted." My words came out in a mixture of anger and sorrow, mixed together in a tornado of pure torture. "Are you even a real person? Do you feel ANYTHING?" I screamed, more harshly than intended, as I saw her cold, callous eyes glaring back at me.

The boiling rage, that had bubbled furiously inside me just moments ago, had begun to subside with each sentence, until I saw we had both pushed each other too far. However, Leila, who had no limits, still continued to scream and shout back at me. Though I had no focus as to what words were shooting out from her lips, I felt the tone

50

of each one like a bullet, hitting me hard in the chest, again and again. I knew Leila had a tendency to go crazy once pushed too far, so I tried with all my strength to conceal my anger and hold back my words, but I saw that it was too late for that. She threw herself towards me and began to release her own wrath through hard, unremitting blows to my stomach, then my arms, until finally, her fist clashed with my jaw, leaving me with an agonising stinging sensation, whilst the taste of blood materialised in the bottom of my mouth. At that moment, I felt a tiny piece of my tooth chip in the collision, though I was in too much shock to pay much attention to it. The air was filled with a deafening silence as we both realised this was the biggest fight we had ever engaged in. For the next few minutes, which seemed like hours, only the sound of our heavy breathing could be heard throughout the large space of the room. I knew, when she saw the blood slowly seeping from my mouth, that she felt sorry, but I also knew her character was so hard, and so stubborn, that I would not be receiving any apology on this day. Leila got up and stumbled into the bedroom, closing the door behind her. Eshta, my little black cat I had rescued from the street, came up close to me, and began brushing his purring body against my leg; that was the only comfort I received, and I had to accept that was all there would be this night. I picked him up, still crying, and held him close, trying to take any warmth and love from this little furry feline that I held so dear. I had a tendency to do this every time I felt lonely or sad; in the end, it always seemed that that cat was my only friend.

That night, the third day of December, I went to sleep in the spare room, alone. It was dusty, and had a peculiar aroma that made it difficult to relax. Usually, Leila and I slept together in the same bed, entwined in each other's arms, but neither of us were about to lay next to the other on this particular night. I lay there in the small single bed that usually remained vacant and unused; there wasn't even a sheet on the mattress, or cover on the bed, so I covered myself with a towel. I lay there, longing for somebody to tend to my wounds – to put their arms around me and tell me that everything was going to be okay. Tightly holding onto the stained pillow, which was worn from age, I began to cry, quietly at first, but then my silent tears turned into a soft wailing that echoed within the walls of that room. The spare room was much smaller than the other one we usually shared; the white paint was chipped in several places, and the air-conditioning didn't function either, which made it disastrously hot within those four walls, particularly during summer months. There was no carpet upon the floor to cover the worn and chipped wooden planks, and we had not swept in several days, so I avoided walking on it without sandals. Loud sobs came from my mouth as I struggled to catch my breath; my body felt frail and tired. I was hungry too, as our fighting had ran into the time when we'd usually eat. Nobody came to me, despite my tears and howling. These past few months, screaming at each other had become normality within our rather curious relationship, but we had never used any form of violence towards each other, up until now. I tossed and turned, but no way was I going to sleep, because, unlike Leila, I had a conscience. Sitting up and pushing the light-blue towel away from my body, I stepped into my white-strapped sandals, walked across the room, and went into the small confinement of the bathroom, where my hideous reflection in the oval-shaped mirror stunned me to full consciousness. The skin around my eyes was puffy and swollen; my face was red and blotchy from crying, and stung as I applied cold water to my skin in an attempt to wash away the stains of our fight. One mark still remained – the blistering redness around my jaw.

'What is this life?' I asked myself in a whisper, drying my face on the sandy-coloured towel that was hung on the back of the door.

The walls were white, not paint, but tiles – shiny, ceramic tiles – each one holding some reflection of a nearby object: a mop, a cluster of shampoo bottles, the towel hung up on the silver hook that had been so carelessly nailed to the door. Everything within the apartment had a carelessness to it, which made sense when we first met the landlord, for he didn't seem to care for much either; his teeth were yellow and crooked, his clothes were two sizes too big and shabby from use, and his health in general was poor. He smoked like a chimney, always had a cigarette in his hand, and, as soon as he had finished one, he would light another. I suddenly had the urge to smoke now, for the stress that was consuming me was overwhelming, and becoming more so with each passing second.

This fight had happened because Leila was pushing me into a relationship I just didn't want to be in, and each day that I had kept silent was a day I had been cut just a little bit deeper. The name 'Mohamed' had become a word I dreaded hearing. When Leila's phone rang out any time, I always knew there was a possibility that *he* would be arriving in the next half hour. When there was a knock at the door, I felt my heart stop every time, for I knew it was *him*. One time, I had even felt physically sick when that dreaded knock had echoed through the apartment. Slow, deep breaths was all I was capable of right now – slow, deep, raspy breaths of shock, sadness, and fear entwined.

Silence. It seemed too silent now. I don't know why, but I had a bad feeling inside me as I sat on the edge of the bathtub; it was a feeling, not of what had happened, but of something more to come. At one point, I thought I heard Leila crying from the other room, but I remembered I was the one that always cried, while Leila usually just screamed and shouted. Standing up again, I turned on the cold water, cupped my hands, and took a drink, before returning to sit on the bath. I didn't know what to do, or where to go. I felt completely restless, and this whole situation just kept gnawing at my mind, like a poison spreading its way through my system.

Why this?

Why all of this?

Then, all of a sudden, I heard it – a horrifying banging coming from the room in which Leila stayed – and, though I really didn't want to enter, my fear for Leila dragged me in there. Despite my quick pace from the bathroom to the room she was in, I opened the door slowly and cautiously, in fear and dread of what was behind it. It was as though time slowed down for a moment, as though we were in the darkest scene of a movie... and then it sped right back up again.

"LEILA, STOP!" I cried, throwing my arms around her, shielding her body with my hand as she consistently hit her head hard against the wall. "STOP!" I shouted again at her. "ARE YOU CRAZY?" My voice came out so high-pitched that I wasn't sure it was even my own, and the word 'crazy' seemed to echo in the air between us. Because all of this *was* crazy; this life we were living, our actions each day, and even, most likely, *us.*

Her face was red like mine, her light-green eyes filled with tears like mine, both old and new, and I realised there and then that Leila was my reflection; we were both crazy, both a danger to ourselves, both in need of the other's love. She was a part of me, and I a part of her. I could see it so clearly now, though I doubted that she saw the same when she looked into my eyes.

"Leila, I love you so much!" I gasped, as though I had just found the answer. "Don't do this... don't ever do this again... please." I pleaded with her, starting to cry once more, staining my face with yet more wet streaks.

Leila's body was cold, shaking with fear, and the adrenaline that had built up inside her. I checked her head with the palm of my hand; she seemed okay – on the outside, at least.

"Drink this." I pushed a glass of water towards her lips; I had found it on the floor beside the bed, and didn't actually know how long it had been there.

She refused at first, but I pushed her to try again, and she took several small sips until, finally, she knocked the glass away and fell into me, clinging to me with her thin delicate arms which, moments ago, had been the cause of my injuries.

This wild and vicious animal that had leapt at me not so long ago had transformed into a tiny cub, in need of protection – protection from *herself*. I loved her so much, but I too was still overwhelmed with anger and distress, and it drained me of all my strength. First the fight, and then the responsibility of taking care of Leila, when I actually needed somebody to take care of me.

Was I even going to receive an apology? I desperately hoped the answer would be yes, but knew that it would not.

I cried, and she saw me, but no such apology came. She didn't ask me if I was okay either, and this upset me even more. 'Why did I continue to love her so much, when she brought me so much pain?

"Lie down. You need to rest," I whispered to her, wanting her so much to calm down, and also wanting to return to the spare room and stay alone. But she wouldn't stop clinging to me, so I stayed.

I stayed with her on the much comfier double bed, stroking her back, soothing her until she fell asleep with me wrapped in her arms, which now seemed so loving.

I was first to wake up the morning after the fight. I slowly moved Leila's arms from around me, wary and tense, as though removing a snake from around my neck, holding my breath as I did so. I left the bed silently, tip-toeing across the wooden floor, departing from the bleak room full of last night's memories. Entering the kitchen, I squinted my eyes, and took a deep breath in and out, before pulling a cup from one cupboard, a jar of coffee from the next, and a packet of milk from the fridge (yes, a 'packet', for the cheapest milk in Egypt arrived in packets). Eshta was there, waiting eagerly to be fed; he always acted as though he'd not eaten in days each time I saw him. He began brushing himself against my ankles, meowing constantly, until I poured him some milk, and cut up some meat for him in his large metal dish. He devoured it in less than a minute, and then resumed following me around the kitchen as I started to make my cup of coffee. It was as though I was a machine, functioning without feeling, though it was still quite early, and my body was numb, my mind hazy. I did actually feel a fraction better this morning, though – this I was sure of – and the scene was much quieter, calmer and stiller; the aftermath always is. Mornings have always been my favourite time of day, particularly when I'm the first wake up. It's like seeing the ground covered with snow and being the first to walk upon it. It's something about the freshness of the air, innocent almost, before any mark has been cast upon it.

I heard a soft creak from the bedroom door, and even softer footsteps that followed, before the hazy outline of her was visible.

"Hi," came Leila's quiet voice from behind me.

She was just waking up too, and smiled at me guiltily as her eyes rested on the redness of my jaw. Her hair was tangled, and she looked exhausted, but her mood seemed calmer, so I held on to this bit of hope.

"Do you want coffee?" I asked her, with a little of last night's sadness returning to me.

She came up and gave me a kiss on my cheek, and then a tight hug. This was her apology. I accepted it.

"I'll make it," she said, releasing me from her arms faster than I really wanted.

"Thank you."

It was strange, the way our moods could change so fast – one-minute hot and the next cold – but this was just how we lived, and there didn't seem to be any other way for us. Leila could be as delicate and pure as winter's first snowflake, or she could be *fire*. It was also dependent on the situation around us – whether Mohamed would be coming or not, though she never linked the two; she idolised Mohamed. I picked up Eshta, and held him close to me, showering him with all the kisses he deserved, as he just rested idly in my arms like he was the most relaxed cat in the world, just lapping up the attention.

"Do you want to go for a walk later?" I asked Leila, as she waited for the kettle to boil.

The sound of its hissing, and the water bubbling inside, filled the kitchen for several seconds, until the loud click followed by a sudden silence announced that it was ready.

"Yes, let's sit and drink coffee on the balcony, and then we can go."

She poured the boiling water over the dark coffee granules, that were mixed with small mounds of white sugar, into two glass cups. We always drank our tea and coffee from glass cups; somehow, it just tasted better that way. Stirring them quickly, creating a light melody each time the spoon touched the glass, she took them in her hands, and walked to the balcony, motioning for me to come with her. I loved that balcony, especially in the early mornings, and even more so when we had hot coffee to drink, and the air outside was warm, yet still fresh. It hovered over a busy street – Nubar Street – and below, we could see the cars queuing up behind each other in an unsightly and unorganised fashion, all honking their horns impatiently, and shouting abuse from their car windows. Leila handed me my cup of coffee, and took a tiny sip from her own as she did so.

"Thank you," I whispered.

As I looked down, I could see an elderly man with a limp washing a car that was caked in mud and dust; he was always there, washing cars, and I think that perhaps that was his job. He was incredibly thin and malnourished looking, yet he scrubbed that car clean with every ounce of his energy. A little further down the road, several large, sandy-coloured dogs were scavenging through a great heap of rubbish for any scraps they could get their paws on; they too looked scrawny and malnourished. The streets were filled with stray dogs and cats, and, though the dogs all seemed to be that same sandy colour, the cats came in all colours and sizes. Nubar street was particularly popular with cats, as there was a small fish market that threw all their scraps away after they had sold the best parts of the fish, and the cats all seem to know the exact time of this daily event. I always found this amusing to watch. Fortunately, we weren't too close to this market; in fact, directly below us was a small bakery, and I could always smell the sweet freshness of baking bread floating up to greet me in the early mornings, just as it did today.

"Are you hungry?" asked Leila, turning to me dreamily, as she too had seemed lost in thought, looking out from the balcony.

I was still surprised at the complete contrast of her from last night. Now she appeared so relaxed, and in the most pleasant of moods. How she did that, I longed to know.

"Not just now. Maybe in an hour or so," I replied, squinting at her as the sun blocked my view.

I saw her only as a dark silhouette, yet her green eyes somehow made their way through into my vision of her, always there, always reminding me that we were the same.

Chapter Four

Summer 2014

One night, after Leila had seduced me into her arms once more, and we were snuggled up close beneath white sheets, she began to show me some photos of Mohamed. The air-con whirred noisily above, creating a more bearable temperature around us, though, each time we turned it off, the heat quickly crept back inside, making it damp and humid once more. I reached for the bottle of water that we always kept in sure supply by the bed, and downed almost half of it in a matter of seconds, as she clicked through the photos, describing the events and scenes in each one. She was wearing a black strapped-top with matching underwear, and her hair was curly and chaotic, quite like my own. She seemed excited at the prospect of sharing these images with me; I could see it in her eyes, and hear it in her voice.

"What do you think of him?" Leila asked me, studying my face as I browsed through them, trying to show as keen an interest as possible.

There weren't a substantial number of photos, but enough for me to build up a picture in my mind of his character; they showed me that he clearly enjoyed playing tennis, his style was fairly casual and sporty, and he had a mass of thick, glossy, black hair.

"He looks nice," I replied, with a gentle smile and quiet voice, to which her face lit up even more.

"I miss him so much," she said. "He is handsome in this photo here," she added, clicking on a photo of him lying on a beach.

I don't know why, but I already sensed that I would at some point meet this 'Mohamed', as we were all based in Cairo, and she was beginning to talk about him more and more as the days passed by. This unsettled me. My experience of men in Egypt was already a negative one, as they constantly hassled me in the street, on the metro, and, even when I stood on the balcony, men below would somehow catch sight of me in a strapped-top, and stare hungrily until I was forced to go inside. Yes, it was safe to say I was uncomfortable at the prospect of getting to know any man in Egypt; it just didn't feel safe. I took another drink from the bottle of water before handing it over to Leila, who drained the remainder in seconds.

"Ah. Thank you," she said, fanning herself with the white, cotton sheet. "You know what I miss? Pepsi."

"We can go out and buy some soon," I said, with a smile. She was obsessed with Pepsi – it was her 'chocolate'.

Me? I preferred the actual chocolate.

Leila spoke on the phone at least three times each week with Mohamed, but they met up only occasionally, for coffee, or a walk in the streets around Cairo. This was always met with great caution, in case they were to run into friends or family. They told me that this would cause big problems, mostly for Leila. I never quite understood what the problem was if they were just walking together, but I just took their word for it, and accepted that things were very different in Egypt; in fact, *our lives* were very different in Egypt.

"Why did you two never get married and live together?" I asked her casually, sitting up on the bed and fanning myself with a leaflet advertising a new pizza shop on Mohamed Farid Street.

She was thirty years old, and I was quickly aware that most women in Egypt would be married and pregnant with their second or third child by now. She admitted that this drew a lot of questions from many people, not just me, and her gaze held a deep thoughtfulness to it that I didn't understand.

"Mohamed doesn't want to get married... and me neither. I don't want to be a housewife and stay at home every day, cooking and cleaning. That life is too boring for me."

I liked how different she was from the majority of women in Egypt, yet I sensed a sadness, or perhaps mild disappointment, when she told me Mohamed didn't want to marry her. I felt then that perhaps Leila did lack this, deep down. As if reading my thoughts, she added:

"Mohamed doesn't like the idea of being bound to one woman for the rest of his life. He gets bored easily and likes to be more adventurous... and so do I."

Her eyes rested on me as she uttered the last few words.

I understood, and felt a little sorry for her, as I saw that hint of sadness linger in her eyes after she spoke the words that no woman on Earth would ever want to have to admit. However, she followed this with a confession which surprised me.

"I cheated on him once – Mohamed," she said, quietly watching me to see my reaction.

She too was sat up now. Reaching over the side of the bed, she switched off the air-conditioning, as the noise

62

was becoming overpowering, and I looked at her to see if she was joking or not. She wasn't.

"Oh... really?" I replied, with wide eyes and a hint of excitement in my voice, as I waited eagerly for the rest of the story to follow.

"He knows about it, and told me that, if I needed to sleep with another man, he would arrange it for me, if that's really what I wanted."

"Whaaaat? No way!" I said, in disbelief that a man in this country could even suggest such a thing to his girlfriend, for I was well-aware of the possessive nature of these men; this definitely didn't make sense to me.

"Really. That's why I stayed with him all this time; because he still loves me, even though he knows I cheated on him, and because he would do that for me."

"Okaaay," I said, looking at her with a puzzled expression, trying to figure her out and make sense of the words I had just heard.

I couldn't help but feel there was something twisted and messed up about what Leila had just told me, yet we left it at that, and I never got to hear the rest of the story.

"Let's go for a walk?" said Leila, as though we hadn't just had the most bizarre conversation in the history of bizarre conversations.

"Okay... and buy Pepsi!" I reminded her.

With that, we both climbed off the bed, onto the ceramic tiles, which provided a much-needed coolness to our feet, and began to get ready to go outside.

***

The following morning, as if by bitter coincidence, Leila received a call from Mohamed. I must have left the room and returned several times before they had finished.

63

It seemed to last forever. As I witnessed Leila's many moods and emotions as they spoke, it was like watching the seasons change, spring to summer, autumn to winter, and then right back to the beginning again. Literally, one moment she would be in tears, and the next she was smiling and laughing, as over an hour passed by, and I actually began to think she resembled somebody suffering from Multiple-Personality Disorder. It was approaching midday, so I began to prepare a fresh salad, topped with lemon juice, salt, pepper, and olive oil. I decided to cook some pasta too, and tomato sauce, as tomatoes seemed to be in good supply inside our fridge. In fact, we had a shelf full of only tomatoes. As always, our fridge was filled with colour, and, once opened, the mixed aroma of fresh fruits and vegetables took ownership over the kitchen. I loved shopping for groceries with Leila, for the markets we went to were so rich in Egyptian culture. There would be large women sat on the dusty ground selling various fruits and vegetables, preparing them as they sat crossed-legged in a shaded area. Leila told me these women travelled from the countryside to sell the vegetables that had grown in their fields, and sometimes men too. Men dressed in long robes, dirty from use, stood behind wooden tables selling tomatoes, potatoes, cucumbers, lettuce, and every kind of vegetable one could imagine; a little further up the street would be chickens, ducks, and rabbits – some in wooden caskets, whilst others just sat there on the tables waiting to be chosen and then 'prepared'. My favourite was 'the carrot man'; he was tall, thin, and his long robes were the dirtiest I had seen, but his smile, his kindness, and his humour always made my day. He sold only carrots, and I felt sure he was very poor, but when I walked on by with my friend, he always said in English "How are yooou?", and then he'd cut and peel two carrots – one for me, and one for Leila. He always laughed and smiled, even in the month of Ramadan, when he was working from the earlier hours without food or water.

Another food place I liked to shop with Leila was this little shack at the end of our street, specialising in herbs and spices. It was the soothing scent of the place that I liked; that, and the variety of fine powders, and oils the colour of syrup. Everything was natural inside and the owner, an elderly gentleman with a grey beard, was so friendly and welcoming; his shop was particularly popular for its herbal medicines that were said to be able to cure any ailment and people travelled miles to purchase them.

Just above my head was a wooden shelf, where a large selection of these spices and herbs were kept in jars, and they always roused my senses as I added them to hot food. I pulled out the ingredients for lunch, and began chopping and slicing until I had a fine variety of foods before me, ready to be served. Just as I was placing everything on the table ready to eat, Leila entered the dining room looking content.

"Perfect timing," I said, placing a dish of hot pasta on the table. "Food is ready."

I sensed a hint of excitement that had not been there previously. She began to plant soft kisses on my neck in such a way that I felt, for a moment, she was trying to seduce me which made me feel slightly uneasy but then she stopped and concluded with a hug – a hug meant for friends – and I was both content and relieved by that.

"So… how did it go with you and Mohamed?" I asked her, as we sat down at the table. I began to eat from the salad bowl, and Leila dished herself some pasta and sauce.

She smiled broadly, and I knew things were good again with them both; she always had a sparkle in her eyes when she thought of him, or when they spoke together. Leila told me how he wanted to try something new in their relationship, as he felt it had become boring of late. He knew that Leila had slept with other men, and this had been difficult for him to accept, because he cared for her very much, and more than any other girl he had known.

"I told him about you and I, and how we are so close," said Leila, looking at me with excitement in her eyes, "and he wants to get to know you."

Leila's hair was fastened back today, and her chiselled cheek-bones appeared higher than I had ever seen them. I had tied my own hair back too whilst preparing the food, as the heat from outside, mixed with the heat from the pasta and sauce as they cooked, was unbearable enough without the added discomfort of long, thick hair wrapped around my neck like a scarf.

Somehow, as I watched her eat, and the way she kept looking at me, I felt there was more to come my way from her conversation with Mohamed, and I was curious to know what exactly it was. I waited patiently for her words that followed.

"He is always saying that he doesn't want a boring life… and he's seen pictures of you, and asked me what I thought about the three of us trying something together."

Leila was still filled with excitement as she spoke, and only now that she had got her words out in the open did she start to relax and breathe. Me, on the other hand? I needed a moment to take it in. In all honesty, her words came as quite a huge shock, but I still loved Leila, and, though she could see I was surprised about the idea, I refrained from releasing any negative comment, for she had a tendency to lock herself in a dark place when something hurt her, and, once she was in that dark place, it was so difficult to get her out of it again.

"So...what do you think, Abi?" she asked quietly.

I detected a hint of hope in her voice, as she spoke like she was a child asking her mother for a new toy. "I know, I know, this is a big question. Just think about it, okay?"

On many occasions, including this one, I felt she just wasn't quite normal in her thoughts, lacking in the normal mannerisms, and I knew from experience that there was no reasoning with her; she could argue that black was white, and vice versa, and to be honest I didn't know what affect it would have if I simply said 'no'. Would she shut down? Would she refrain from speaking to me? Would our friendship end right there?

The strange thing about my friendship with Leila was that sometimes it was calm and beautiful, just like the river Nile, but other times it seemed there was an unspoken tension, and Leila would change slightly. We left the subject open for discussion, and resumed eating lunch. I smiled at her, and she smiled back at me, reminding me just how happy I was, living with her in the centre of Cairo.

"Do you want to go for a walk?" I asked her, after we had consumed most of the food, and were now clearing away the dishes.

"Hmm, okay. Where do you want to go?" Leila replied. "Do you wanna go night-time shopping? And we can go get ice-cream?" she added, smiling; she knew I loved it when we walked around the shops at night, and she knew how much I loved the ice-cream in Egypt.

I nodded my head in excitement as I carried the final dishes into the kitchen, filled the sink with warm soapy water, and began to wash up.

"Okay. Let's clean up, and then we can head out," said Leila, grabbing a cloth and wiping the sideboard clean.

Eshta rubbed himself against me, informing me that he was hungry.

"Move, Eshta!" scolded Leila, as she almost stood on him.

"Aww, he's hungry," I said, immediately opening up the fridge to tend to his needs.

Leila laughed and shook her head, but Eshta was happy as I placed down a generous portion of meat.

It wasn't until much later in the evening that we finally made it outside, as we had been distracted by various household tasks, and then a movie had appeared on the television that had captivated us. It featured Julianne Moore, and told the story of a woman who suffered from Alzheimer's disease at quite a young age; it was quite a sad movie, but captivating all the same. We eventually left the apartment at around 8.30 in the evening, and found ourselves walking down Sherif Street, and then towards Talaat Harb Square, where we admired the glittering, silver jewellery through the window of one of our favourite shops, Ali Baba. The door was propped open with a wooden chair, so we stepped inside to take a closer look. Leila asked the price of several pieces she liked; one was a silver chain, with some Arabic writing hung from it, which Leila informed me said 'Allah'. The gentleman was polite and patient as we viewed one piece of silver after another, and, even when we didn't purchase anything at all, his face was kind as he told us he'd give us a good price if we changed our minds. It was around nine p.m. now, and the street was quite dark, yet lit up by the glow of artificial lighting that came from shops, bazaars, and cafes, all clustered together like a parade of night-time madness (particularly with the noise, and the constant chatter of a foreign tongue I still had not digested.) The street was full now of families out shopping, and enjoying their outings together. I particularly liked to see the women in their long flowing robes and head scarves, because, even though they had to cover their body and hair, they would make up for this by dowsing themselves in perfume and heavy eye-liner, topped with bright red lipstick – yes, we women always find a way to express ourselves in some form or another. At the end of this long and busy street was a shop called El Abd, which was always swarming with people purchasing cakes and ice-cream like there was no other shop selling such delights. This was the shop where we bought our two scoops of chocolate and vanilla, in a small carton. It was the small things, the little moments with Leila, that reminded me of why I stayed with her, and why I loved her so much. It wasn't usual for Leila to be sensitive and loving on the outside, but, when she was, it was so sweet, and I just wanted to hug her. And I did. It was a wonderful night, just Leila and I walking hand in hand down the quiet streets, talking, laughing, and being completely relaxed in each other's company. It was one of my favourite nights.

As we lay in bed together that night, I felt I wanted to show Leila just how much I really loved her.

"Yes. I'll do it," I said quietly, without further explanation, and she didn't require any, as she understood what I meant.

"Thank you," she replied excitedly.

Although I had agreed to this, I don't think I ever really thought things through properly. In fact, my 'agreement' seemed almost an impulsive action, where I only considered how much I loved Leila, and felt I owed her the world. She filled a gap within me that I'd had since childhood, and that was huge for me. I did owe her everything, because what she had given me was in fact everything I had ever desired, ever needed, and spent a lifetime searching for.

It was just after six p.m, and the sky was steadily turning darker, as I stood on the balcony for a while, collecting my thoughts. There were those sandy-coloured street dogs again, three of them searching for food in the large heaps of rubbish. I smoked one of my slim Karelia cigarettes – an Egyptian brand I had taken a liking to. I favoured the slim ones, for they made me feel somewhat more elegant, and I guess they were healthier in some respect too, due to their lower levels of tar, nicotine, etc. I often smoked too much when I was feeling nervous, like now, for instance, and the box was close to being empty. There was very little breeze, and the air felt sticky as I continued to look down at the busy street below. A pile of cars was building up as all the men tried desperately to return home, and a recurring honking of two or three cars worked its way up to my ears. Men in worn, discoloured gallabeas puffed on cigarettes, whilst drinking dark tea; no wonder their teeth were always brown and crooked. I took one puff after the other of my more elegant, and healthier cigarettes, and then stubbed it out on the balcony wall. Having avoided the approaching moment for as long as I could, I worked up the courage to go back inside and start preparing myself in a way that I felt was expected. I found some pretty clothes – clothes I thought they would approve of, rather than clothes I favoured – choosing a silky, red strap-top and some black fitted trousers to go over my carefully selected matching underwear. I knew it would be more important what I was wearing underneath, yet that thought alone sent a shiver down my spine.

"What time is he coming?" I asked Leila, as we both stood in the mirror, applying copious amounts of make-up like two young girls preparing for a party.

Leila appeared much more excited than I did, as she spritzed herself with numerous perfumes, and applied more eye-liner than usual. Earlier in the day, she had waxed almost every area of her body, including her lower back and upper lip. This amused me, though it was one of the only things that did throughout that day.

"I don't know. He said he would call me when he sets off from his house," she said, checking her phone to see if there were any messages or missed calls. "You look nice," she said, with a sweet smile.

"Thanks."

I still wasn't exactly sure how I felt about this whole ordeal; I was nervous of course, a little afraid too, but I guess there was a tiny element of excitement at the prospect of Mohamed coming over, and all three of us sharing this experience together. It was something new and crazy, though it seemed to me that somehow the cultural stereotypes had been switched dramatically within this situation. Westerners have always been viewed as being much more liberal, whereas those from the East were strict, conservative, and traditional in their ways. Yet here we were, in the pit of this unlikely scenario, with no idea as to where it would lead.

It was seven p.m. when he finally arrived at the door. He was bearing gifts of chocolate and, to my surprise, a bottle of wine, like a real gentleman – an English

71

gentleman, almost. So, on his part, our first meeting was pleasant, and so was he. I didn't understand the wine in the beginning, for they were both Muslim, and I knew that wine was forbidden, but it turned out that it was Leila who had asked him to bring it. The evening was already full of bizarre surprises before it had even truly begun – wild, unexpected surprises. We talked a little together, all three of us, though Leila had to translate throughout the evening, as my Arabic was poor, and so was his English. Mohamed was giving me more attention than I had expected, and it was the intimate kind – planting nice comments in my ear at any opportunity, sometimes accompanied with a gentle touch, or a soft stroke of my hair. I felt flattered by this, though it wasn't long before desires became actions, as we began to kiss and touch each other, and my anticipation grew. Leila and Mohamed stood up, as though this was the 'planned' moment. They led me to the large bed in the next room, that was usually meant for Leila and I, and then he removed his shirt. Leila kissed him, and simultaneously began to remove her clothes, before motioning for me to do the same. They helped me. I was nervous and rigid in my movements, though Mohamed did his best to help me relax. Leila just seemed wild and ravenous; she was different. Mohamed gave Leila and I an equal amount of attention, kissing one and touching the other, whilst we both applied ourselves to him and his needs. From the outside, I imagined that it was *seductive* and *erotic*, but unfortunately my emotions did not correspond with this perception, and I felt that I took very little from the experience that night. It neither aroused me nor touched my heart, but I made them feel otherwise. I felt I needed to do that; I didn't want to hurt or offend either of them. This was my first mistake, but I did it out of love for Leila, and fear of hurting her – or

72

worse, losing her. I have always had a tendency to put myself through pain for the love of another, even when it wasn't necessary. Maybe it is just another way to sabotage myself – I don't quite know.

"I'm so happy," whispered Leila.

"Me too," added Mohamed.

I knew this was the moment I was supposed to say 'me too'; I knew because they were both looking at me, waiting. So, I gave them the words I knew they wanted.

"Me too," I said quietly.

After we had done the deed together, it seemed we were all relaxed and happy, so we had a little drink from the wine.

"For you," said Mohamed, handing me a half-filled glass.

"Thank you."

Leila had already poured her own, and there we were together, sat on the bed sipping wine, two perfectly happy people… and me.

"Do you like it?" I asked her.

"Hmm, a little, but I don't feel anything."

I knew she was referring to the dizziness she had heard about, yet never experienced.

"I really want to be drunk," she added.

I laughed, and so did Mohamed, though I noticed a look of concern on his face. He was just wearing his boxers now – black ones that went well with his dark skin, and even darker hair. Leila was also in black underwear, though her skin was much lighter than his, and her hair was a dark brown, whereas Mohamed's was jet-black, shiny, and well-styled. Looking down at my own skin, I was such a contrast to them; I was as white as a snowflake and, ironically, my underwear was white too – the complete opposite of theirs.

Leila moved towards Mohamed, rubbing herself against him as though she were a cat, and he returned the gesture, putting his muscular arms around her. I sat there, wondering if I should leave and give them some privacy, but even that didn't make sense at this point, as I had just slept with them both. Instead, I tried to remain calm, appear happy, and do as was expected, all the while feeling lonely, and completely betrayed by my best friend.

"What time is it?" asked Leila. "I'm so tired."

"After one a.m.," replied Mohamed, stretching out his arms. "Shall we sleep?"

"I'm actually kind of tired now," I said, gathering some of my things that had become scattered around the room: my phone, sandals, and the top I had been wearing.

"Okay," said Leila, with a relaxed stretch, and a smile that showed she had taken everything she had wanted on this night.

Mohamed and I moved first, and prepared to sleep, whilst Leila lingered a little longer. We imagined she was just cleaning up, however she had in fact stayed to drink the remaining wine. I guess it was the excitement of drinking alcohol for the first time, and later she did explain that she just *really* wanted to feel what it was like to be drunk. I was English and could accept this, as I had been in her position many years ago, though of course Leila had not really had the opportunity before this day. She came to join Mohamed and I without saying a word. She lay down, and we all start to sleep, though within moments she was up again. As if we were all inside a movie playing in slow motion, Leila began to make a scene before our very eyes.

"I feel ill," she said in English, though the rest of her words that followed were in Arabic, and I couldn't understand. Leila climbed out of the bed and wandered around a little in such a disorientated fashion that I felt the need to follow her. Mohamed staggered behind us a moment after, first into the living room, and then the bathroom.

I was tired, and felt a wave of anger at her, though I chose not to express it. We were both disappointed in her, Mohamed and I, though we helped a drunken Leila into bed once again, so she could sleep it off. However, after perhaps thirty minutes or so, when all was quiet, Mohamed thought she was sleeping, and so did I. Which I guess was why he began to give me more attention as we lay there together. And I let him. First, he began by stroking my arm, and then kissing my neck, moving closer to me beneath the sheet. I was still exhausted, and my mood was becoming darker with every passing moment, but still I let him... until suddenly, Leila got up fast, staggered across the bedroom, and went to the other room, sobbing hysterically.

"What?" I said, shocked and worried, jumping out of bed immediately, swallowing my own pain to quickly tend to hers.

Mohamed and I followed her into the living room, where she was sat on the floor crying; she pushed me away. She pushed me away hard. Mohamed ushered me away, politely, yet still the action brought with it a pain, anger, and sadness that I once again had to swallow. They spoke in loud, hysterical voices, whilst I waited just outside the room, shaking, crying – not really understanding. Time passed... too much time. They finished talking. Leila hugged me. Mohamed hugged the two of us. We went to sleep.

That night, Leila made me feel like I had betrayed her; yet, on the inside, I was still struggling to come to terms with this 'wonderful' thing I was trying to do for her. In theory, she had betrayed me, yet I didn't know how to express this, so I held it inside. She apologised the next day, of course, but, as much as I loved her, I guess I never really accepted that five letter word from her: 'sorry'. I suffered greatly, and that night remained a scar that would stay with me, perhaps for the rest of my life. Despite this, it wasn't the last time we would sleep together, the three of us; it became a repeated affair. I became weaker, Leila became hungrier, and Mohamed just kept getting luckier, gaining more and more each time.

Chapter Five

London, March 2015

Today there were five yellow roses displayed in the glass vase on the table between us, and, as I inhaled deeply to see if I could steal away any of their scent, I just couldn't help but notice how beautiful and perfectly formed each flower was. I couldn't find any flaw in them; each one, though slightly different to the others, was a rose in its own right – natural, innocent, and fresh, without any desire to be anything other than a rose.

Victoria sat there, with perfect posture, taking notes, whilst I delivered broken fragments of my past that once again caused me waves of anxiety, mixed with that familiar ache and longing. However, to my relief, she didn't judge me. She never judged me, just as she had said in our first session. She looked at me one or two times as I spoke, and held her gaze for longer than I felt comfortable, but her face still bore no obvious expression. Instead, she helped me when I found some of the more intimate details difficult to speak about, and she told me how well I was doing each time I struggled to catch my breath. I had been seeing Victoria weekly for over a month now, so today was my fifth or sixth visit. However, I still did not feel that we had made any significant progress. Most sessions passed by almost the same as the last. Sometimes I saw her twice in a week, sometimes just the once; nonetheless, I still didn't feel any less pain in my heart. I still cried most nights, and I was still vomiting and self-harming on a weekly basis. We seemed to have drifted away from my Bulimia, and were now focusing a lot on my friends in Egypt, and the *odd* relationship we'd had. I didn't really understand why – did she think they were the cause of my *abnormality*? I still didn't fully understand what my *abnormality* even was. Right now, for me, I could only describe it as a mixture of crazy emotions – ups and downs – and a difficulty in differentiating the past from the present. But I felt I needed something more official – a label that explained it all. It was as though this was the missing piece. How I longed to be one of those simple, yellow roses!

"I heard that the fights in Egypt became so bad that you all decided to separate. Could you tell me a little more about that?" she asked, as she sat there perfectly poised, legs crossed, with her hands clasped together, resting on top.

She was giving me her undivided attention. Nobody had ever done that – not in the way she was doing right now – and it made me feel somewhat important, like I mattered, whereas my past had always suggested the opposite.

I thought about those fights, and the overall craziness of them. The way they would continue days on end, and the way we would miss meal after meal because of them. I lost a lot of weight because of those fights, though it crept back on the happier days. I remembered how both mine and Leila's face-shape changed dramatically when we fought for several days at a time, as the weight just fell off us, almost by the hour, and the stress brought with it dark circles and added lines. As I reminisced on those tragic moments, an image suddenly appeared in my mind of the spare bedroom in our apartment in Cairo, and the dusty, wooden flooring that constantly needed to be swept. When the image faded, I was aware that I had been staring at the polished laminate flooring in the room where Victoria Green and I were currently sitting. How curious, the way a memory can be triggered from the slightest similarity, like how a colour, a particular scent, or sometimes even certain foods could remind me of something from Egypt.

I looked up at Victoria.

"Well, actually, this happened many times; many times we decided to split. But there was something in all of us that always wanted to try again. It became like an addiction – a ferocious circle that had no hope of ending. I realise the preposterousness of it all, really I do, but I feel like I need Leila in my life. She's my family."

As I spoke, I fiddled with a silver bracelet fastened around my wrist; it had tiny green gems entwined within the silver swirls, and it was my favourite bracelet. It was my favourite because it had been a gift from Leila. She had bought me it for my birthday. We'd had a fight that day, and she had left me alone crying for hours on end, yet I wore that bracelet as though it meant something – that perhaps she cared. I don't know why I wore it.

"Okay," said Victoria, and she fixated her gaze on me in a somewhat concerned expression, and intrigued, in the sense she felt she might be onto something. "So would you say, even though you could see and feel that the relationship was broken, that you had/*have* a tendency to try to cling onto those broken pieces?"

I thought about her words before answering, looking for a hidden meaning, treading carefully, though, when I was satisfied that there was none, I nodded my head. "Yes. And as I said, I *need* Leila."

Her name echoed in my thoughts until I found those familiar tears trickling down both my cheeks. "I need Leila." I repeated the words as though she might hear them, and come waltzing through the door at any moment. "I need her so much."

"It sounds to me like you grew very dependent on Leila," she said quietly.

I just sat there and cried, whilst Victoria watched me with interest. I noticed she was wearing a dark-grey suit today, as opposed to her usual black attire, and her dark hair had a soft kink to it – a calm wave, almost. She edged closer, handing me a tissue, and with it a gentle smile.

"Thank you," I said, taking the tissue from her, and holding nervously onto the hem of my light-grey, woollen jumper, scrunching it tightly and releasing it, repeating the action as though it had an aim. "Yes... I think I was dependent on her. I think this is why I found it so hard to leave the relationship, despite the fights, and the control, and the whole messed up scenario."

More tears streamed down my cheeks. I couldn't stop them. She saw I was struggling.

"It's okay. You can cry in here, it's alright." Her voice was soothing, something I was grateful for at that moment, though it wasn't the voice I wished to hear.

"Victoria, I feel completely lost. I'm scared, and I don't know what to do. I'm really scared," I said, my voice unsteady, as were my two hands, which I moved frantically in time to my words, expressing the despair in which I was trapped. "I just don't know how to live my life anymore. I feel like something is wrong with me."

I realised how I must be coming across to her – like an overdramatic and hopeless romantic – but I couldn't help it. I *was* an overdramatic and hopeless romantic.

"What do you feel is wrong with you, Abi?"

"I don't know. I just feel... different."

For a brief moment, I considered reaching over to hug Victoria, to hold on to her in the hope she would return the gesture. It wasn't out of affection, but more from desperation – desperation to feel another's touch on my own body, desperation to be inside somebody else's arms, and to feel secure. I did not act on this thought.

"We will figure this out together, and in the meantime, you have my support, and the support of your sister."

I nodded my head, for I knew she was right.

"It's okay to feel lost. Everybody feels this at some point in their lives, but you will find your place in the world again, and, if you work with me as you are doing today, I can guarantee that you will find it soon."

The one positive thing about these sessions was that I was finding it easier to confide in Victoria – much more than during that first session, anyway. This was a kind of breakthrough in itself, for I hadn't been any good at talking to anyone since my return from Egypt. Even in all the time I had spent in my sister's house, we weren't actually communicating with each other. It was more like we just existed around each other. Sure, we asked 'How was your day today?' and 'What do you want for lunch?', but we weren't talking about the important things. There was always a sad, little wall between us – one that neither of us knew how to overcome. Nonetheless, I knew that she wasn't going to let any harm come to me while I was under her roof. This gave me comfort.

"I did grow quite dependent on Leila," I said, once again answering the question that had been asked earlier. "I relied on her to translate everything, to take me places. If she wouldn't go, then I wouldn't go, simple as that. I wasn't like that in the beginning, but... I guess I grew more and more fragile as time went on, and the situation became... well... as it did." I stopped to take several deep breaths before continuing. "Also, in Cairo, in Egypt in general, it's not easy for a young woman to walk down the streets without being hounded and harassed by the men. Even the Metro has segregated carriages – one for women and others for men." I fiddled with my hair as I spoke, wrapping the loose curls around my fingers, then releasing them again, though I quickly became bored with this activity and just pushed my hair behind my ears. I began fiddling with my watch instead.

All the while, Victoria was watching me with great intent, focusing on my body language, and the words that came from my lips in a voice that shook as though I was cold. She watched me as I kept staring at the yellow roses, the painting on the wall, and the window just behind her chair. I think my story intrigued her in some way, and I imagined none of her other clients would be delivering such a curious tale as mine, though I was open to the possibility that I could be wrong.

"Would you also say that you are afraid of being left alone, Abi?" asked Victoria.

This time, when she spoke, there was an air of sympathy in her voice that I clung to, as though she had given me a great, big hug, strong and tight like the ones Leila would give me each night. Leila and I must have hugged each other at least five times a day. *Five*; there was something about that number that always remained with me. It had a significance that I was aware of, yet didn't always understand. The number five had been ingrained within me. Had it been because of the prayers?

Had their religion somehow taken over a part of me?

Should I still pray?

I started to feel water returning to my eyes, and, simultaneously, I began fidgeting on that blue-cushioned chair, trying desperately to disguise my agitation and discomfort at the question. Loneliness was perhaps my greatest fear, and my hugest heartache, and yet I didn't even realise it fully until now. This made me feel all the more vulnerable, as I glanced at her nervously, the lady who seemed to know more about me than I did. Broken fragments of those times in my life when I had expressed fear of being alone suddenly formed in my mind, one after the other, as though it were a dark slideshow. There were so many of them. I had been an anxious child at school, and then at college, and thereafter, though it had improved a little with age. But, during my time in Egypt, my fear and anxiety had reached a dangerous height; I was consumed by it. Perhaps the problem had always been there, since childhood, but the events in Egypt had acted as a kind of trigger, digging everything up, forcing it to the surface. All those deep-rooted issues had now been *de-rooted*.

I took a deep breath.

"Yes," I replied, so softly that my voice seemed to quiver within the white walls, the floor, the blue chair beneath me, and the light wooden table that was so well varnished, it reflected the fluorescent ceiling above.

"It's okay, Abi," said Victoria, offering me a gentle smile, and encouraging me to continue.

Sadly, for the both of us, I could not.

"I'm sorry," I whispered.

Nonetheless, there it was, as clear as the light of day: the inner beautiful part of the woman sat before me. It shone out in the softness of her voice, and the empathy within her brown eyes, that, in the beginning, I'd felt had held no warmth. A part of me still wanted Victoria to reach out, wrap her arms around me tightly, and tell me everything would be okay, but I knew that, in the real world, that would never happen. She was a professional, and she would never be able to be my friend, and for the briefest of moments, a wave of anger crept over me – anger at her not being able to offer me any friendship, when that was the thing I craved the most.

"I'm sorry," I repeated, wiping a tear from the corner of my eye.

I wiped my tears on the sleeve of my jumper. The wool was soft and comforting, like a child's blanket, though I sniffled a little too loudly whilst trying to recompose myself. I crossed my legs, and uncrossed them again, several times during my discomfort, causing the hem of my black trousers to rise and reveal my suede shoes, that were also black, the colour of mourning. They were beautiful, high-heeled, shoes that I had bought in Cairo around four months ago, and I could still remember the shop, as though it were only five minutes ago that I had handed over two hundred Egyptian pounds to the sales assistant. He had been an elderly man, who hid behind a thick, prickly looking beard, though I knew there was a kind smile beneath it. Thinking of Cairo didn't help me – it only made my being here all the more agonising – yet I couldn't think of anything else. Here I was, sat across from Victoria, all the while wishing it were Leila I was looking at, wishing the weather was much warmer so I might not require this heavy jumper I wore, and wishing just to walk on the bridge over the river Nile and meet her for the first time all over again.

"Here, take a tissue; wipe your face." She held the box before me and I extracted several tissues.

She offered me space in the form of silence. Not an awkward silence, but a comforting one, though it was during that soft, tranquil, quietness in the room that I suddenly longed to see outside the window. I longed to see something natural – a tree, a green field, or flowers that grew from the ground – but it was too far away from where I was sitting, and was positioned behind Victoria. She was unknowingly blocking my view. I looked through her. I imagined a serene, green park, perhaps with a small stream, and some ducks too. I saw the ducks splashing their little webbed feet in the water, pushing their fat bodies from one end to the other. I saw the water's surface glittering beneath the bright sun, and I saw an elderly man with thinning hair, and a woman equal in age, walk on by, hand in hand. Then, as if by sheer magic, I saw *her*. There was a figure in the distance, dressed in beige trousers and a red, fitted t-shirt, an outfit I remembered so well. It was Leila, though the scene around her was no longer the greenness of the park; instead, there were the sandy stones beneath her feet, and dust – mounds of dust – sweeping through the air. The weather was hot and sticky, and Leila was walking towards me, waving, beckoning me towards her.

"Abi!" A distant voice suddenly reached me, pulling me away from Leila, pulling me back to that room, and reluctantly I followed the sound of my name.

It took me a moment to remember where I was, to gather my surroundings, and see that Victoria was there, watching me with concern, curiosity and, if I was not mistaken, pity.

85

Had she seen her too?

"Sorry... I..."

I had always been a daydreamer, 'away with the fairies' as some kindly put it, though I guess when you are a woman aged twenty-seven, suffering from repeated trauma, the fairies no longer exist, and the problem becomes psychological.

"Does this happen often, Abi? Do you find yourself unable to remain focus?"

"Erm. Yes, I suppose I do have a lot of problems with focusing," I replied, feeling confused and slightly emotional at having seen Leila right here, during my therapy session. However, I realised how bizarre and strange I must be coming across to her, so I made an extra effort to focus and cast aside my daydreaming.

"I am just wondering; what you were thinking about, Abi?" said Victoria, offering me the chance to tell her, but without asking me directly.

"I was thinking about Leila... in Cairo... I felt kind of like I was there. It felt so hot, the weather – just like I remember."

She nodded thoughtfully, and jotted something down in the notebook she always had close by. This time, for almost an entire minute, she scribbled down various words, whilst I just sat there, staring at the white wall to my left, becoming more and more lost within myself. I fidgeted on that blue cushioned chair as though it were filled with crawling insects, and, once again, I crossed and uncrossed my legs, as I so often did when I felt nervous. Repeating this action brought me no comfort.

"What's wrong with me?" I asked, interrupting her note-taking. "I want to know what's wrong with me." My voice was childlike and pleading.

She didn't answer, and this made me angry.

"I need to be okay again. Help me," I begged, with an air of desperation in my voice I had not yet used with Victoria.

"I know you want a 'quick fix'," she said quietly. "and if I could give this to you, I would."

I felt my patience melting away into a hot lava that seemed to be flooding the floor of this heated room. It was slowly moving in on me, ready to eat away at my feet, which were fixated firmly on the floor. My face felt hot, and my eyes stung from previous tears.

"I can't be like this!" I stammered, as though she hadn't said anything to me. Perhaps I hadn't heard her; perhaps I was incapable of listening to her just now. I didn't know; I was only aware of my own desperation, confusion, and incapability.

The palms of my hands felt sticky, and I suddenly felt a huge surge of anger, though whether it was at Victoria or myself, or at Leila or Mohamed, I just didn't know. I knew only that it was boiling over, and it needed to spill out from its container.

"What's wrong with me?" I said, much louder this time, determined to get her attention, though the moment these words had shot from my lips they turned to sobs – loud, unremitting sobs.

She looked at me, in the calmest possible way, yet with friendly, sympathetic eyes, and told me again that I must be patient. She promised she would help fix me.

"Abi, what you are feeling is completely understandable with what you've been through; you are dealing with a lot just now."

I continued to cry. I turned away from her, to conceal my pathetic, wailing face from hers, which was so beautiful, and unstained by tears and rage. There had been many times in my life, just like this one right now, where

I had been suddenly unable to control my emotions, my anger, my tears; everything would just come pouring out. Normal people express emotions in a variety of different ways. For children, it's the easiest; they can scream, shout, laugh, and cry, and it's okay. But, when you are an adult, it's no longer considered to be acceptable or normal. Why were my emotions always so extreme?

"I don't like to give anyone a label unless I feel it would be beneficial, but in your case, I do feel it would be of some help – have you heard of the term 'Post-Traumatic Stress' before?"

I shook my head, though tried to stop my crying so I could focus on her words.

"Post-Traumatic Stress occurs when a person experiences a traumatic event, which can be in a single moment, or over a prolonged period, as is the case with you. Some of the symptoms involve flashbacks, where it is as though you are reliving the event, or at least similar feelings as you had during that time, such as fear and anxiety." She stopped, looking into my eyes to check I was following, and that I could handle this information.

I nodded, and urged her to continue, eager for a deeper explanation, whilst feeling that this all made so much sense.

"Also, the individual might suffer from insomnia, be constantly on edge, and may even engage in some form of self-destructive behaviour."

I nodded again, not because I wanted her to continue this time, but because what she said sounded familiar to me: the insomnia, the self-harm, flashbacks. I appreciated the label, for it helped me understand a little more about myself and what I was experiencing. That night, I would research this further. I thanked her.

"Abi, did you ever self-harm while you were in Egypt?"

Chapter Six

The next morning, Mohamed reluctantly got up for work, kissing us both softly on the cheek before he left, whilst Leila and I remained in the comfort of the bed, wrapped in soft, white sheets. Now it was just the two of us, she snuggled up to me, kissing me, touching me in a way I didn't understand, yet, at the same time, didn't care to. Whatever way she touched me felt okay with me, just as long as it was her and not him. The moment Mohamed left, I immediately felt more relaxed and relieved, as my body, which had been tense for most of the night, now allowed itself to sink into the softness of the mattress. I lay there, just thankful that it was over, that I had survived another 'trauma', and, perhaps more quickly than normal, I cast the event out of my mind and began to focus on the present. Leila hugged me tightly, then pressed her face close to mine, planting tiny kisses on my cheek, and then, amidst it all, we both burst into a muffle of giggles beneath the sheets, until it became too hot, and we had to come up for air. It was as though nothing out of the ordinary had happened the previous night; I suppose it was becoming more 'normal' between us. I was starting to get used to the pain.

"What do you want to do today?" I asked her sleepily, allowing my eyes to remain shut just a moment longer, savouring the sound of our laughter and the tightness of her hug.

I felt slightly nervous about opening my eyes, just in case any of last nights' pain might be visible in them, and I figured the longer I kept them shut, the easier it was to remain in a dreamlike state of denial. I needed to maintain my current calm state, my *happy* state.

"Hmm, I don't know," she replied softly. "We could go buy some groceries."

I felt her sit up in the bed beside me. She rested her hand on my face and, just like that, I felt my anxieties melt away. Now I could open my eyes. Leila had that effect on me; she could wound me deeply, but ease the pain just as quickly through a simple and kind gesture. Her touch on my face was like a 'mother's touch': deep, consoling, and loving. She was my protection from all that was bad in the world.

I too sat up beside her, with a smile creeping up on my face, slowly, like the rising of the sun, until it had fully formed into a beaming grin.

"Yes! Good idea! Let's go," I said quickly, through a series of giggles, throwing the covers off us both and jumping out of bed.

I took Leila by the hand, pulled her off the bed, and urged her to get dressed quickly.

Whenever the prospect of 'going outside' was broached, whether it be for long walks, shopping trips, or exploring new areas, I always felt such a surge of excitement run through my veins, and right to my heart, for I loved the outdoors. Cairo was still fairly new to me, as I had only been there a matter of months, and there were still many districts, towns, and villages waiting for me to discover them. Leila was the best tour guide, always taking me to the most interesting areas.

"Ohhh," groaned Leila, staggering around the room in a dreamlike state.

She was clearly hoping for a little more time in bed, though she was smiling at my bouncy, childlike manner that had made a sudden appearance.

"Come on… let's go, let's go," I urged her more and more, until I had succeeded in waking her fully. "We need to shower."

"Yes, come on," she laughed.

We showered together. It was nothing of an intimate nature when we did this; sometimes we were just like two sisters who felt completely relaxed in one another's company, splashing around like two children. We hardly even looked at each other. After cooling off beneath the cold water for a few minutes, we got dressed, both in jeans and a top. It was quite hot outside but, due to the sea of men that constantly swam around us young women all day long, we did attempt to cover as much as possible. I tied my hair back whilst it was still wet, and Leila did the same, as it would help us stay cooler for a little longer beneath the hot sun. Both of us automatically applied eyeliner to our faces, as we did every morning. Leila had always worn it, and I had become accustomed to it purely from spending time in a country where women loved eyeliner.

"Okay, we can go to the market at the end of Nubar Street for vegetables, and then Masreya Supermarket for meat and coffee, and… we will see after that," said Leila, calculating what shopping needed to be done.

I grabbed the keys, slipped into my sandals, and said 'goodbye' to Eshta, who was already purring for food. We had run out of his favourite meat last night; he'd only had milk since we had woken up, and gosh was he making me feel bad about it.

"We need to get meat for Eshta," I reminded Leila, as we departed from the apartment, down four floors of chipped, concrete steps covered in dust, and out of the building into a cloud of heat.

"Oh, you think more about Eshta than us!" said Leila, shaking her head.

"I love him; he's family." I laughed. "Oh, what about bread?"

"Ah yes, we will go and get bread right at the end."

Egyptian bread, which was baked in a special kind of factory, was transported and distributed throughout the city by young boys on bikes, in such an amazing way that I often stopped whatever I was doing just to watch. Balancing large trays made from woven wood – three feet long and two feet wide – in one hand, they would steer the bike with the other, moving with caution through the street. It was quite a talent, and I knew nobody in England would be able to do this. This bread was extremely popular, for it was eaten with almost every meal, every day of every week. We would wait in line beneath the scorching sun to take ten or twenty pieces of this flat, round bread from a lady called Mona. The cost was one Egyptian pound if we were taking twenty pieces; this was equivalent to ten pence in England. Despite the overwhelming heat in the summer months, I liked Cairo, mainly because everything seemed to be about twenty years behind England, which just made the whole way of life so much simpler and more relaxed. There were still men who worked in the streets, taking little money to shine people's shoes. Large carts of fruit were pulled by donkeys, which were led by old men wearing long robes, and often a turban too. Meanwhile, the women from the

93

countryside would sit in the street, selling home-grown vegetables. I liked this – I liked all of it. I loved the dusty, sandy atmosphere that was always visible; I loved the sun and the heat it brought; I loved the chatter of Arabic that filled the warm air, and I loved Egyptian bread. Like any city, however, it did have its negatives too; for example, there seemed to be no set price in shops, so good bartering skills were essential, and also, nobody seemed to respect time, hence the forever popular reference to 'Egyptian time'. For Leila, this was all very normal – it was just everyday life – but, for me, each waking day was a grand adventure, with new discoveries, and visual delicacies for my eyes to devour, topped with new experiences for my memory journal. The challenges, too, were never in short supply. Even our overall living arrangement had become one of those adventures for me; well, at first, that's what it was, the idea of it anyway, though I guess over time it became a *challenge*.

As much as I loved being in Cairo, surrounded by its intense culture, the bigger problems soon began to emerge from within our household. We now shared the apartment together, the three of us, and I saw less and less of just Leila, and more and more of 'Mohamed and Leila'. Slowly, day by day, I was becoming isolated within a torturous triangle, not even by Mohamed, but by Leila. She was pushing me out without even realising it, hurting me without even feeling it, and standing by while I began to fall further and further down that black hole I felt would soon become my home. We slept in the same bed, and I watched as they snuggled up together each night. Mohamed always tried to draw me into that human-mound, though, once he'd fallen asleep, I always removed myself from his arms. I would turn and cry into the pillow, silently, like an unfelt breeze passing over a deserted town, covered by a heavy blanket of bitter darkness. I cried because he was there, and his presence unsettled me. I cried also because of the dramatic change in Leila; he affected everything that was once natural, happy, and bright, and when he touched it, it became dark. I felt it each time he touched me.

I often thought about how I could banish myself from the situation, but, each time I thought of leaving, I was overwhelmed by the fear and sadness of not having Leila; I was becoming dependent on her. I was becoming more and more vulnerable with each passing day, and there was nothing I could do to stop it.

It was Wednesday evening when we had the fight – an unforgettable fight that hit me like a bullet. She had promised me that we would go out somewhere, just me and her, and spend some quality time together, but of course, when Mohamed arrived, she was swooned into staying in bed with him and cancelling our plans, like every time. In fact, it had become something expected by now – the cancelling of our plans for 'sex'. She had already begun to apply make-up on top of the eyeliner that was always there. She sprayed herself with a musty perfume that he had bought her, and began to style her mass of dark hair, fastening it back with numerous clips.

"Leila, you promised me," I pleaded, my teary eyes following her around the room like a lost puppy.

I really missed her, despite being in the same apartment. I just didn't get to see her as much as before, and I was starting to feel desperately alone and isolated within the white walls… within Cairo. In Cairo, it is not easy to meet new people when you don't speak the language, so Leila was my world, whereas I seemed only to be her other *option*. I now felt scared to go out alone without her, but scared to remain inside with the two of them. I was trapped, and fully aware of it.

"But Mohamed is here – we can't just go out when he arrives."

"Leila! He *arrives* every day," I stammered, becoming frustrated at her constant let-downs; I was always being pushed aside to make way for *the king*.

We were trying to keep our argument as low-key as possible, so as not to disturb him whilst he waited on the bed in the other room.

"I will stay in this room tonight," I said solemnly, no longer able to continue this same old conversation, knowing she was never going to show me any remorse or kindness.

"Fine. As you like, Abi." And with those final words, which stung my ears like a thousand angry bees, she walked away.

I slammed the door shut in anger, and burst into tears, though, within seconds, the door swung open again in such a vicious manner that I knew something bad was coming.

"Don't you DARE slam the door!" she screamed at me, pushing me hard into the wall, her hand clasping my jaw so tightly I felt everything inside begin to crush slowly, as I struggled to retrieve the air lost within my lungs.

I screamed silently, yet wailed loudly, as my body hit the wall several times. Mohamed appeared with a look of shock and anger on his face. He pulled Leila into the other room whilst she was still shouting, and thrashing her arms in the air like her body had been taken over by a demonic creature. Meanwhile, I was left alone. I expected somebody to come to me that night – to apologise, to ask if I was okay – but nobody came. I waited and I waited, but it was once again with false hope. Pain, sadness, and loneliness took over my body. I felt weaker as the minutes turned into hours.

That night, I crept past the room which they were both in; they had the door closed, and, as I listened outside for a brief moment, I was mortified to hear that they were in fact having sex. I was so hurt by the fact that I had been abused by Leila and she had been rewarded with sex from Mohamed; how could she? How could she hurt me like that, and then have no sense, no conscience? And HIM... he clearly didn't care about me either. Why was I still here?

I stepped into the kitchen. The white tiles felt cold against my bare feet. Eshta was sleeping in a corner he had taken a liking to, though even *his* presence could not take me out of my current state of sadness. I quietly took the knife with the orange handle from the drawer below the sink. Eshta looked up, but didn't move. I left as quietly as I had entered, though I did not dare to listen outside the bedroom door again. Instead, I returned to the spare room, sat on the dusty wooden floor, not caring how dirty it made my clothes, then, almost automatically, I began to cut at my arms – quick, unremitting slashes – until the pain came, followed by the tragic flow of blood, dripping slowly down my arms like a freshly cut stream. There it was – a beautiful, tranquil flow of liquid, running slowly down my wrist, onto my hands, ending at the tips of my fingers. I watched, and I imagined my pain disappearing with it.

Chapter Seven

London, April 2015

A tiny beam of light had begun to creep across my bedroom floor, in the same way a single drop of water seeps through a fresh sheet of paper, slowly giving life to every piece of furniture and object within my surroundings. Despite the warm heaviness of my thick quilt-cover, and the comfort it provided, the sun was beckoning me to wake up. I yawned and stretched, allowing everything to whir into focus, and, just then, I realised I felt such a sense of possibility in the day that lay ahead of me. A day with no mistakes in it, no stains – it was fresh and new as a baby straight from the womb. Climbing out of bed, and walking swiftly towards my window, I became conscious of the fact that I hadn't felt like this in such a long time; there was a certain spring in my step that hadn't been there before.

Was I recovering?

With one quick tug, I had opened the curtains and allowed the sunlight to fill my entire room, and oh how bright it shone! In fact, right there and then, I felt the need to open the window, lean out of it, and inhale the freshness of the early morning air. As I did so, my curls danced in the light breeze, whilst the sound of birds singing mixed with a passing car formed a unique morning melody – one which I felt deserved to be danced to.

'What a beautiful day,' I thought to myself, slowly pulling my head back inside.

I went to the bathroom, where its whiteness only added to the air of positivity and hopefulness, and then, as I turned on the water, and removed my white robe, I remembered Leila. I remembered how we used to shower together on days like this – sunny, warm days – before Mohamed came onto the scene. I had always felt so comfortable with her; there was no shame, no awkwardness, nothing negative in our relationship. No label fit the way *we* fit together, but that was okay; who needs a label when you have each other?

All that really matters is that you yourself understand it, and enjoy all those connections, feelings, and emotions that grow from it. I missed her.

Putting aside those past memories, I stepped into the shower, allowing the hot water to fall onto my bare skin; it always made me feel so relaxed, and this morning was no exception, as warm mist filled the bathroom until the entire scene was a blur. I applied white, scented soaps to my body, and then allowed them to be washed away, until I felt I was clean, and my skin felt smooth. Then, once I had finished, I stepped out through the fog, and only my memory led me to find the towel hung on the back of the door. How beautiful this morning was; I couldn't quite believe it, for it had sprung from nowhere, unexpectedly, like the sun from behind a dark cloud. When I returned to my room, a light humming from somewhere within my bed caused me to go into a frantic search amongst the cotton sheets, the quilt cover, and through a pile of clothes left carelessly on the end of my bed. I knew what this sound meant before my eyes had even confirmed it; I saw it there, my phone buzzing, and a familiar face flashing on the screen. My heart skipped a beat upon receiving that confirmation; she still had that effect on me, even after everything that had happened. The photo which I had selected for her calls was one I had taken in a seafood restaurant that we had eaten in together; she was wearing a light pink blouse, and her hair was left loose and curly. I answered it after the fifth ring, in a voice that portrayed every ounce of my happiness, eagerness, and love that was always there beneath the surface.

"HI LEILA!" I said, rising up from the bed, and straightening it out once more with the palm of my hand.

I walked across the deep-red carpet towards my window, and ran my fingers over the beige curtains that I had previously opened; they instantly reminded me of Cairo, and its overall beige, sandy colour.

"ABI! How are you?" came Leila's own voice, which was filled with an equal amount of excitement to my own.

I dried myself as I spoke with her, and vigorously released my hair from the confinement of the towel, sending a cascade of water onto my carpet that immediately darkened in colour.

"I'm okay," I said softly, tilting my head to one side.

Gazing up at the sky through the window, I focused on the sun, imagining myself back in Egypt in the apartment we shared, with the air-conditioning whirring noisily around us. I imagined Eshta, my little cat, walking across the bed to prop himself on top of me, as he so often did.

"How are you?" I asked, sitting down now, so I could apply my full attention to the call – to Leila.

"I'm okay. Eshta misses you." Her voice quivered.

She had kept Eshta after I left, promising to take care of him, stating that he was 'part of me' so she would love him always.

"Oh, how is he?" I said, my voice turning high and excited, as I suddenly felt he was near.

"He's okay – eating meat as always."

We laughed at the image, though I just wanted to hold him again, and it saddened me that it wasn't possible. I stood up and paced around my room, not really knowing what to do or say, for nothing felt right, nothing felt appropriate, as I began to sob silently.

There was a silence before either of us spoke again, yet I was surprised that it was Leila who filled it.

"I miss you," she said quietly, and there was a sincerity in her voice that made me imagine her expression sad, and eyes filled with water, just as mine were right now.

"Me too."

Another silence. I swallowed hard, returning to the window, my eyes fixated on the street below that suddenly seemed so grey and dull, despite such a sunny start.

That's all it took – one fleeting moment for my feeling of happiness to dissolve.

"What are you doing these days, Abi?"

I had already given her a brief outline about how my sister had made me see the psychiatrist, to which Leila had laughed, saying that I didn't need any of this; I just needed to come back to Egypt to stay with her and Mohamed again. I don't know why, after everything that had happened, we were always so willing to throw ourselves back into the same turmoil and chaos, but that's how it was with us. Maybe, on some level, we were all crazy, though it was only me that was in therapy right now.

"I have an appointment with Victoria again today." I let out a little laugh, though inside I was not amused at all by my situation. But talking with Leila *did* make it seem a somewhat lighter issue in my life.

"Come back to us, Abi," said Leila, in a soft, pleading voice more suited to a child. "Mohamed said he wants to give us another chance. This time it will be different."

I shook my head wearily, raising my eyebrows at the preposterousness of the situation, and at Leila's sudden calmness. She was a lot like the ever-changing climate in England; she could resemble a violent storm, and then transform to sunshine and breeze within an instant, without warning, just as it might do today.

"I want to… really… but I have the doctors and things here, you know."

"You don't need a doctor, Abi!" she said firmly.

I knew that Leila would just give me the answer that suited her. She would easily tell me I didn't need a doctor, just so I would come back and stay with her and Mohamed. That was what she did – thought of herself – and I needed to accept that. Even though I was fully aware of this, I felt myself been lured into their web; not forcefully, however… almost *voluntary*. I mean, what else did I have going for me here, besides doctors, therapies, and so on? It was hardly a life. It wasn't a life I seemed to be able to accept, regardless of it becoming a necessity for me.

Just then, as my mind was being swayed gently like the trees outside, my sister popped her head around the door, and motioned to me that she had prepared breakfast for us both.

"Wait just a second, Leila," I said, before covering the phone.

"Okay, Helen, I'll be down in five minutes."

Helen frowned slightly, once she knew I was on the phone to Leila. She disapproved, of course, and I understood why, but I also knew she did not understand anything about me and my needs, or the kind of life I had led over in Egypt. She left the room and I heard her footsteps on the stairs, growing softer, until I knew she had gone.

"Who was that?" asked Leila.

"My sister. I have to go; she made breakfast."

"Okay. Do you miss the Egyptian bread and foul?" She laughed, knowing how much I loved the bread and detested the foul.

Foul in Egypt was what the poor people ate, and consisted of brown beans in a similarly brown kind of water, however Leila always mixed it with a large dollop of butter, and a generous sprinkle of salt, making the taste much more pleasant. Nevertheless, it wasn't the dish I would ever choose.

"Haha, just the bread, Leila – you know."

There was another silence where I smiled at that tiny fragment of memory she had presented me with, and I knew she was doing the same, even though we were miles apart and in separate countries. I was smiling, and so was she.

"I love you."

"I love you too. Talk soon, Leila."

"Okay, bye. Big hug."

"Bye."

I took a deep breath, and swallowed hard, trying to fight back any tears that might be lingering. I loved her so much, and I knew I always would, but was she damaging me even more? The answer, I knew, was most likely a big, fat 'yes', but it had become like an addiction, and I felt soon I would be drawn back to Egypt. I felt soon I would be ready to do this all over again. How long could I last without Leila? Then again, how long would I last if I went back to Leila and Mohamed?

Was I using them as another form of self-harm?

Switching myself to my current reality, I left my phone on the bed, wrapped my dressing-gown around me, then put on my fluffy, white slippers and walked downstairs. In the kitchen, my sister was just pouring our tea into two delicate china cups – cups, I noticed, that had belonged to our late grandmother. I stepped closer to where my sister was, and smiled at the beautiful breakfast scene she had carefully set up for us both.

"I didn't know you had these," I said, holding one in my hands, admiring its intricate design, and savouring sweet memories of our dear grandmother.

"Yes, I took them after she died, when we were clearing out the house. I have some of her jewellery too, if you want to choose something for you to keep as a memento?" said Helen, seeing how happy I was at the sight of the china cups.

"That would be nice," I said, though my mind had begun to drift back to the conversation with Leila and 'Egyptian bread'. "Aww, you made breakfast like Grandma used to, too."

There on the tray, which was ready to be carried to the dining room, were two boiled eggs, salt, pepper, and toast cut into five little soldiers. We always ate in the dining room; it was where the small, round, wooden table was, accompanied by two matching chairs. My sister wasn't famous for entertaining guests, nor did she have much time for it, but I liked our meal times together, even if they were brief. I placed the tea and the two eggs, both in their hen-shaped egg cups, onto the table, then sat down with Helen to eat.

Our Grandma had been a special figure for both my sister and I growing up; for me, she was the one part of my childhood I could say was normal, and filled with a genuine love and affection that only the dearest of grandmas could provide. We always spent the weekends with her: she cooked Sunday dinners to absolute perfection, she took us on fun day-trips to the seaside, indulging us with ice-cream and other sugary treats; and she also took us to church every Sunday, where we were taught about God, and how to live a good, honest life. She was truly amazing.

I dipped a soldier into my egg – it was warm and runny, just the way she used to make it.

"How's your work going?" I asked, offering some light conversation to accompany our breakfast.

"Fine. The students are sitting their exams in these weeks, so my work load is lighter, thankfully," she replied, before putting an elegant spoonful into her mouth.

"Hmm, good."

"Have you thought what you are going to do about a job yet?" she asked me.

I looked up, for her question surprised me; I hadn't even thought about getting a job here. In fact, I didn't even know if I wanted to stay, though I chose not to voice this, as I didn't want to ruin the current scene of tranquillity set before us.

"I don't know. I don't really feel there is anything I'm good at." I sighed. "Maybe I will find something in a shop until I make my mind up."

Helen nodded in agreement, and continued to eat her egg and soldiers. When we had both finished, she went on to clear the table. It took me back again to when we'd finished breakfast with Grandma, and how she used to take the table cloth to the front door, and shake it so the crumbs fell onto her perfectly mowed lawn. Afterwards, we would all stand and watch as the birds swooped down to devour the tiny meal we had left them. I wished for this moment to go much slower, for it was pleasant and calm. However, the clock continued to tick, until I heard the distant sound of Helen's voice calling me for the next appointment with Victoria.

"I'm ready," I said, as I joined her once more at the top of the stairs. "Let's go do this!" I added, with a voice full of enthusiasm and sarcasm mixed together.

She frowned at me. "Come on."

Down the carpeted stairs we went, and out of our shiny, white door that, despite the usual grey, English weather, always seemed immaculately clean, compared to everything else around it. I knew Helen to be quite obsessive about tidiness and cleaning; in fact, I often wondered if she had an Obsessive-Compulsive Disorder, though I thought it wiser not to voice this thought.

"Your hair looks nice – did you do something different?" asked Helen, studying my curls.

"I washed it," I replied, with a light laugh.

Today, I could feel the cool air on my face as I buried myself in my beige, tartan scarf and black fitted coat; it must have been around ten degrees at least, and the sky had already changed from blue to grey, and back to blue again. I had my umbrella with me, dangling freely in my hand, for there was still no knowing what the weather had in store for us during the next hours.

"Hey," said Helen, stopping in the street just a couple of minutes from the Health Centre; "I meant it when I said you should choose some things from Grandma's stuff."

I smiled at her. "Thanks. I'd love to have a look through them when we get back."

We continued down the street, amidst the noise of traffic and the distant chatter of men, women, and children out walking, each travelling to their own destinations: jobs they either loved or loathed, the supermarket to do the weekly shop, or out walking their dogs. Everyone was moving, and it felt good to be part of that – to be doing what other people were doing, and to not feel so abnormal and different to them. My sister kept glancing over at me as we walked, perhaps out of concern, or maybe just to check I was still there, though, once the large building with its shiny, glass doors came into focus, it was time for her too to leave. She rubbed the side of my arm, as though warming me from a cold breeze, and then wished me luck.

"I'll leave you here, okay," she said. "See you later, Abi."

"Bye," I called, as she turned and began to walk in the direction of her work, for that's where she was heading now.

I watched her, just for a moment, until she was merely a perfectly poised silhouette in front of the sun, which had just appeared again. Despite us never having being incredibly close as sisters, I had felt a wave of comfort pass over me as she had rubbed my arm and said goodbye.

I entered the building through the glass doors, which opened automatically as I approached, and took a seat in the blue-carpeted waiting room until I was summoned. There were around ten chairs, though they were made of a hard, grey plastic, unlike the one I sat on when I saw Victoria, and there was a small table too, featuring some magazines. Most of them seemed to show celebrities on

107

the cover, but this didn't interest me, for I had been away for so long I barely recognised them anymore.

"Abigail. Hi."

My name was being called. I looked up and it was Victoria. She was beckoning me to follow her into the white room to begin this morning's session.

"How have you been this week?" she asked, as she led me down a small corridor, and into that same room, which was becoming like a second home.

She was dressed in black again today, just as she had been for the majority of our sessions, and I began to wonder if she was perhaps portraying her own inner depression through her clothes. With a tiny smile of amusement, I answered her question, and told her how this week had actually been quite pleasant, and that I'd been in contact with my friends from Egypt. I told her I was thinking of going back to them.

"Oh?" Victoria looked at me with a concern that I hadn't seen before, nor had I ever expected such a sentiment, for I was aware that therapists, doctors, and nurses never *really* cared about the individuals sat before them; they just pretended, because it was their job. "So the relationship between the three of you is ongoing?"

I wasn't sure if I was imagining this or not, but it seemed almost as if Victoria was portraying a sense of displeasure at my life in Egypt, and also seemed surprised by the fact that it was, in fact, 'ongoing'.

"Of course!" I replied obstinately, "they're my best friends!" I was starting to feel a tiny spark of resentment, as she didn't seem to understand the seriousness of our relationship. "I love them and miss them!"

I fidgeted in my seat, fixing my gaze on the glass vase, which, for the first time in all my sessions, did not contain any flowers.

Why were there no flowers in the vase?

I wondered if it was meant to be symbolic of something – a feeling of emptiness or loss perhaps – or whether she had simply forgotten.

Victoria sat before me bearing no obvious expression, yet I sensed she was about to challenge me. But maybe I only sensed this because, on some level, that was what I too was doing; I was challenging myself. Part of me knew what I was doing was preposterous and completely irrational, but the other part – the stronger part – just wanted to be right back there with Leila.

"These people, the ones that pushed you to self-harm, and leave the country to stay with your sister... *these* are your 'best friends'?" she said, in a calm tone, but slowly, as though she required me to think carefully about each word.

I noticed she had put emphasis on the word 'these'; she wanted me to think clearly. But I *was* thinking clearly, wasn't I?

The room went quiet, and only the white walls seemed to speak, uttering words like 'crazy', 'abnormal', 'deluded'. Despite the resentment that had risen inside of me, I decided to try and conceal it, for I didn't want to humiliate myself anymore, or give her the pleasure of seeing me react. However, when I looked up at her, we were suddenly caught in a fierce lock: a battle between our eyes, a staring competition that I vowed to myself I would not lose. I saw Victoria's eyes were a dark brown, strong and determined, yet somehow compassionate at the same time, whilst my own light-green eyes were angry, but weakened by my hurt, and seemed to struggle to maintain focus. After merely a few seconds, I felt the water forming in the bottom of my eyes. I held my breath, hoping that the water would not leak out and start running down my cheeks, but it did. Like raindrops running down the glass of a window, one after another, they came.

Why was I determined to cause tension between myself and Victoria Green?

I didn't want to, I didn't mean to do it, but I couldn't stop myself; it was as though, when I saw she was trying to help me, I felt the need to push her away as hard as I could. It was like another form of self-harm, because, afterwards, it was me that suffered, not her.

"I want to leave," I said, standing up and moving towards the door. "I can't do this today."

I knew from experience that sometimes it is better just to walk away than to confront, however, to my surprise, she stood up too, much more calmly and composedly than I had done, of course. It was almost as if it were the end of the session and she was going to walk me to the door, though she didn't do this. I started to move quickly, because I was nervous, afraid, and agitated all at once. I had already grabbed my coat and scarf when she asked me, in the calmest of voices, to wait, and to try again.

"I'm sorry, Abi, really. Let's lessen the pace a little. How does that sound?"

She told me I needed to be patient for this therapy to work. Then, to my surprise, she told me again that she was sorry for her strong approach, and that she would be gentler with her words from now on. I told her 'okay', and then, slowly and reluctantly, as though my legs had suddenly increased in weight, I returned to my seat. We looked at each other for a moment – her with the same sympathetic eyes, and me with a much more vulnerable gaze than my earlier one, which had been filled with anger. Placing my beige scarf and black coat back on the chair arm, I took a deep breath, and then presented her with a tiny smile; I was showing her that I was ready to

110

try again, and also that I was sorry for my reaction. Victoria returned the smile; she was showing me that she wasn't going anywhere.

"Abi, can you tell me about when you over-eat and then make yourself sick, so we can try and recognise the triggers of your bulimia?" asked Victoria softly. She even accompanied her question with another gentler, and more sympathetic, smile, which seemed to dilute the harshness of the words 'bulimia' and 'sick'.

I don't really know why, but I found it quite easy to talk about my bulimia; it seemed such a minor problem compared to everything else. Was that crazy?

Maybe.

"Well... it's a mix really. Sometimes, when I am angry or upset, I will binge and make myself sick. But then, sometimes, it seems completely random, and I will do it without cause – like a routine, almost."

She nodded, as though it were an answer she had expected to hear, and took some notes, which I imagined she would read through later. Pushing her dark hair behind her ear, Victoria looked up at me again, urging me to continue.

"I noticed that 'change' seems to be one factor that can trigger it. If, for example, I have planned my day out, and then somebody arrives at the house who I haven't been expecting, or I don't really like, then this has often been a trigger."

"Somebody like... Mohamed, when you were expecting a day alone with Leila, perhaps?"

Now it was my turn to look up at her: 'Wow' I thought. "Yes. Exactly like that."

"Okay." She nodded. "That makes perfect sense, and you seem to have identified a key trigger there."

Her eyes portrayed such a clear sense of empathy that I couldn't help but hang on to the hope that another person understood just what I was feeling beneath the weight of my words.

"Bulimia is often a result of being in situations that one cannot control, yet has a 'need' to control. And, from what you have told me, it seems that you did need to maintain, or get back, some of that control. This was just your way of coping. It was what you needed to do... to survive."

Using only my eyes, I tried to communicate to her my gratitude over what she had just said, for her words touched me, and made me feel more normal – stronger even – as she described me in some way as a 'survivor'. I liked this. It appeared that a wave of understanding had just passed between us, and this felt incredibly special. I looked at her, communicating my inner secrets through my eyes, and she looked at me, responding, telling me that it was okay to feel what I was feeling, and that it *was* going to get easier. Unfortunately, that pleasant moment between myself and Victoria Green was brief, just as my pleasant mood earlier that morning; as quickly as it came, it disappeared again with her next question, which roused those anxious feelings that were always lingering just around the corner, waiting to pounce.

"Is it true that, several months ago, when you were in Egypt, you had to be hospitalised for attempted suicide?"

Chapter Eight

Cairo, November 2014

A pool of Arabic words swam around me as I lay on the thin, leather mattress, which was covered by a stained, white sheet. Every sixty seconds, I reached for the bowl beside me, violently releasing the toxins from inside my thinning body. I was injected with something by a man in a long, white coat, then I vomited again... and again... and again. He gave me some pink medicine to drink; they told Leila that it would make me bring up all the medicine I had taken – she translated this to me. I vomited some more – the pink liquid bubbled and fizzed in my mouth, and, the second it ran down my throat, it came right back up again. My throat burned now; the muscles in my stomach were exhausted from all the contracting, as I purged another time, violent vomiting that I could not control. It was as though my body had taken on a life of its own, contracting, pushing, heaving – emptying itself of the poison that had been put inside... that I had willingly put inside. A wave of dizziness took over my entire body, and all I could do was lay there, until I would need to reach for the bowl once more.

Mohamed and Leila had grabbed the nearest taxi and taken me to hospital. Most of it was a hazy blur to me, but I remember seeing a sign in English that read:

NATIONAL POISON CENTRE. I wondered if they had told the doctors I had attempted to take my own life, for I knew it was a sin in Egypt; only God can give and take a life, as Leila had so bluntly stated to me. Mohamed had appeared much more frightened than Leila, once they had understood what I'd done, and this surprised me; he had been the one to take charge of the situation and summon the taxi, shouting at Leila in Arabic, though about what exactly I didn't know. I was shaking, crying, and confused, as I was moved around from pillar to post with no real idea as to what was going to happen to me. The hospital was completely unsanitary, worryingly so, and the doctors were all male of course: tall, dark skin, and black oily hair, speaking in Arabic, moving around quickly, grabbing various tools and instruments.

My suicide attempt had come about much in the same way as when I had self-harmed; I hadn't even thought it over that well, I had just gone downstairs in my pool of sadness, entered the nearest pharmacy, and purchased a cocktail of medicine: paracetamol, co-codamol, and sleeping tablets. And then, whilst crying in the spare room that I sometimes slept in when Mohamed was present, I began to swallow them whole. At first, I did not even require the aid of water, but then, as my throat began to feel dry and unable to let them pass, I went to the fridge and washed them down with an orange liquid I could not taste. Both Leila and Mohamed had come into the room several times, and had just assumed I was tired, as I was laying on the bed, eyes barely open (though later, when my body reacted and the vomiting started, I had had no choice but to tell them what I'd done, as they questioned me over and over in their own confused state.) By evening, I was crying out for help, for the pain in my stomach was becoming unbearable, and that's how I came to be in the hospital. I didn't know whether I wanted to die or not – in fact, my thoughts had changed several times throughout the day, once I'd already taken the medicine. What I was sure of, however, was that I desperately wanted to escape the situation I was in. I needed to get out, and maybe dying *was* the only way out. For the time being, I was willing to put my life in somebody else's hands, and let them make the decision, because one; I did not care anymore, and two; I didn't feel mentally able to take charge of my own thoughts, decisions, and actions. I was slowly losing my sense of being – my identity – and that inner strength I had always had. It had been growing weaker for some time, losing its elasticity, slowly dying.

A doctor told Leila that I should remain there in the hospital overnight, but she said 'no', and, when she translated this to me, I was incredibly relieved at her response, as the prospect of remaining in that unhygienic, run-down hospital, swarming with Egyptian men in white coats, brought a raw fear to my bedside that was much deeper than not waking up at all. I would never have survived. Mohamed had had to pay the doctors money for treating me, though he had told Leila not to tell me how much, and it was moments like this that made me feel he cared for me more than Leila did. The whole situation was becoming more and more confusing to me each day. I loved Leila, Leila loved Mohamed, and Mohamed loved both of us.

After six or seven long and torturous hours, we returned by taxi to the apartment where it had all begun; my body was weakened, frail, and tired. Mohamed went out to buy food, and Leila stayed with me in the bed, cuddling me back to full health. I was so weakened from the event that I could hardly lift my own body, or drink from the glass of water that had been placed beside me. Leila made sure I took all the right medicine that had been prescribed by the doctor; she calculated how much time passed between each dosage, and she stayed by my side throughout it all. It was so strange that night, for Leila was a complete contrast to the selfish and angry character she had been showing me; in fact, her taking care of me throughout that event became one of my happiest memories in Cairo. I had felt so safe in her arms, and when she was at the hospital organising everything. I knew she wouldn't let anything bad happen to me; she had everything under control. We lay on the bed together, both in the spare room, and she told me how everything was going to be just fine, as I sank my face into the light-blue sheets to keep warm. They carried a scent of someone ill having stayed in bed for a long time, but neither of us had the energy to change them on this night, so we just dealt with it quietly.

"I love you, Abi," whispered Leila softly. "Don't do this again, okay?"

I responded by squeezing her arm, and she hugged me tighter, a hug in which I felt so incredibly safe.

Eshta, who was still so small, came and sat on the bed with us, purring quietly, and soothing me into an even deeper relaxation that I welcomed. Leila told me that, when I was being sick, she'd also found Eshta doing the same in the kitchen, and we joked that he was copying his momma. I think I had drifted off into a light sleep when I heard Mohamed return. He popped his head around the door, and saw our eyes were open, so he came up close to me and showed me what he'd brought: a large, cardboard box with the familiar gold writing – 'Etoile'. Etoile was the cake shop he had taken us to on several occasions, and, as he pulled open the box, we saw it was filled with a dozen intricately designed cakes, drizzled in white icing and chocolate swirls, filled with thick cream that Leila and I, and even Eshta, had always loved. It had always been considered a 'treat' when Mohamed brought us cake, however, though it was a seemingly kind gesture, he clearly did not understand how bad I felt inside due to the overdose as he urged me to eat one. They looked delicious, yet I couldn't even manage to put one forkful into my mouth without the thought of vomiting again; I told him I would try one tomorrow. Somehow, and with great difficulty, I did manage to eat half of a cucumber that night, with a sprinkle of salt, whilst Eshta munched away on a new box of meat, especially for him. That little cat from the street always brought me so much joy, especially in my darkest hours; I found humour and love in everything he did. Another unexpected pleasantness that came from the tragic incident that night was that Leila stayed in the spare room with me to sleep... and I slept like a baby in the arms of a mother. Mohamed had told her to stay with me; even though it would mean that he stayed alone, he knew I just wanted to sleep with Leila, and he allowed it.

Chapter Nine

London, April 2015

Helen appeared so much more relaxed in her casual attire, as she placed the DVD into the player, and turned up the volume. Dressed in a pair of loose-fitting, navy-blue trousers, and a light-grey t-shirt with a foreign logo on the front, she was a complete contrast to her usual sophisticated self; even her hair was swept back into a loose ponytail, as opposed to the more complicated styles she wore for work.

"I think you will like this; it reminds me a little of you," she said, glancing at me whilst she fiddled with the remote.

"Oh… okay. I hope it's nice." I laughed.

I too was dressed in casual clothes: a comfortable pair of leggings and a loose, white jumper, perfect for an evening of lounging around the house and watching movies. I stood up from the leather couch, took the lighter from the coffee table, and began to light some candles. I had always loved candles and the therapeutic mood they created; my sister shared this love with me, hence the reason the wooden table, mantel piece, kitchen, and bathroom were flooded with them.

"Can I light this one?" I asked, motioning to one of her more expensive Yankee candles; it was vanilla-scented – my favourite.

"Yes, sure," she replied, smiling that I was showing an interest in something other than my past traumas. "Do you want popcorn?"

"Yes, that'll be nice," I replied, returning to the comfort of the couch, and taking hold of the remote, though, after a few seconds, I jumped back up again, following my sister to the kitchen, the same way I used to follow Leila each time she went to cook something.

I still missed her, and found memories of her lurking within every task, scene, and object throughout each day, whether it was the familiar scent of a candle, certain flavours in the foods I ate, or a simple action done by my sister. Leila was everywhere, in everything, and there was no escaping this.

"So, what's the name of the movie?" I asked, opening the cupboard and taking out a bag of the tiny yellow corn, whilst Helen found the bottle of oil, and a metal pan with a lid.

"Into the Wild. It's actually based on a true story. An adventure. Do you want salt or sugar?"

I used to love sugary popcorn, but since spending so much time with Leila in Egypt, and eating mostly salty foods, my taste buds had re-adapted to match hers.

"Salt," I declared with a smile.

"Salt it is."

She drizzled the oil into the silver container, whilst I lit the stove. Light poured into the kitchen from the window, causing me to squint each time I walked past a particular part. I liked how it caught the red glass of the fruit bowl, making it sparkle against the wall. I began pouring the corn inside the silver pan, and then, after less

119

than a minute, they began to hit the lid like tiny hailstones hitting the window on one of those stormy winter days. I liked the sound it made, like a foreign music without any real direction, aim, or rhythm.

When we returned to the living room, the vanilla scent from the Yankee candle had taken over the air, and my sister's ornaments and vases seemed to dance on the walls behind the flicker of all the other candles. Helen had closed the curtains, so it appeared warm and cosy as we sank into the comfort of the couch. Within minutes, we were completely engrossed in the movie, and the adventure of a boy who seemed so full of life, so sure of himself. It was a pleasant moment that we shared, munching on more popcorn than our stomachs were able to obtain, whilst engaging in the story of the young boy who really was a lot like myself. It was an enlightening and emotional account of how he didn't feel he fitted into society, and survived outside, in the wild, travelling and enjoying nature. It appealed to me in every way; she was right in the sense that he was like me, or I was like him, and also that I would like this movie. I was happy that we had found time to relax together, Helen and I, and to share something ordinary that had no relation to therapy or Egypt; this moment was long overdue.

***

I chose to wear black like Victoria; I wasn't in mourning or anything, I had just always liked to wear dark colours, and clearly so did she. I sat opposite her, waiting for the array of questions she would deliver during this session, and realised that I didn't feel as nervous as I usually did, which I think was because I was starting to relax in her company, and see her less and less as the villain I'd first portrayed her to be. These sessions had been ongoing for almost four months now, and, in some ways, that white room with the blue-cushioned chairs had become a part of my life… and I was okay with that. Victoria opened up her laptop, and removed her coat to reveal her usual black leggings, and the pair of high-heeled, black suede boots she had worn often, and that I liked. Her fitted, grey top was quite stylish too, and something I would definitely purchase if I earned a salary anything like hers, for it was clearly designer. She was the perfect portrayal of a classy, elegant lady. The room seemed a little cool today, as it was early morning, and the heating had been switched off all night, so I kept my own knee-length black coat on, but opened it to avoid getting hot once the conversation started. It always made me nervous and clammy when Victoria started digging into my personal life, picking at the twisted contents of my brain, and trying to make sense of them before I even could. Some days, I did wonder whether she was helping me at all, or causing more damage that was yet to be undone, and, in my whirl of paranoia, I was constantly on edge, expecting her to send me to a psychiatric hospital at any given moment. However, I was always honest with her when I spoke – not that I felt I had much choice in the matter, for Victoria Green seemed to possess a power over me, and I felt sure that, if I lied, she would know immediately. Deep down, I knew she *was* helping me, more than I cared to admit; I suppose I just struggled with the idea of her, this woman who was not my friend or my family, yet she seemed to possess healing powers, and she understood me.

"How are you feeling?" she asked me, keying in the password on the laptop, which I thought was sleek and stylish, just like her.

121

"Fine. This last week was quiet, uneventful," I said.

"Good, that sounds more optimistic at least." She smiled. "Today, I want to move away from our usual conversation about Egypt, and focus a little on your family history. So, I'm going to be asking you some quite personal questions, and I would appreciate it if you could answer as truthfully as you can, okay?"

"Okay," I replied.

'Quite personal questions – well there's nothing new there!' I thought to myself, with an inner frown that may have shown on my face.

"How do you feel about that – discussing your family?" she asked, which I appreciated, for it was as though she was giving me some control over the session.

"I'm okay with that." I smiled weakly. "Though I don't expect it to be easy. That's if I can remember enough, as I think I've blocked a lot of it out over the years."

"Okay, well, if you feel it gets too much at any time, just tell me, and we can come back to it another day. You mustn't feel pressurised to talk about anything that you don't want to."

Although I felt her words were kind, I couldn't help but feel a little lost at the prospect of taking control of the conversation; perhaps I was slightly dependent on Victoria, just as I had been with my 'friends' in Egypt.

"Thank you," I said, my eyes scanning the white walls absent-mindedly, distracted only by the tiny cracks in the paint, as though they were tiny obstacles put there to prevent me from moving on again.

She took an elegant sip from her bottle of Evian, positioning her lips lightly on the rim, and tipping it gently; she was so calculated and precise, even in the simplest of tasks. I did quite like to watch her and analyse her, I realised, as I gazed at her putting the lid back on using her thumb and index finger, revealing a set of well-manicured nails I hadn't noticed before. The tiniest of things could capture my attention; one time, I had become engrossed in watching a tiny spider weaving a web just outside my window; I had stopped what I was doing and watched it for over fifteen minutes.

"Could you briefly outline the relationship between you and your family, and any particular memories that stand out for you?" asked Victoria, so eloquently, and in such a perfectly calm tone.

I almost longed for her to slip up, as her perfection was beginning to irritate me on some level, though perhaps that was just because she was everything I hoped to be.

My eyes studied the pot of pens and piles of paper, neatly organised on her desk, whilst I tried to buy myself some time to answer such a big question.

'Where would I even start?' I thought to myself, as I struggled to evoke the distant images of my mother and father.

Slowly, and with great effort, they whirred into focus, and all of a sudden I felt sad and weak, just as I had done all those years ago. My head was filled with shouting, swearing – plates being shattered as they flew through the air.

Screaming.

Crying.

Pleading.

More crying.

"Well..." I began, searching for the words inside, though my emotions and thoughts seemed so noisy and catastrophic that finding the right words proved to be quite a difficult task.

I didn't particularly want to travel back there, for it was a deeply painful period in my life, but I knew, as always, there was no avoiding anything with Victoria, especially if I *wanted* to recover, which I did.

"It's safe to say the relationship wasn't a pleasant one." One deep breath. "My *mother* was a senseless woman: cold, almost dead inside. She used to over-medicate a lot too." I hesitated, and took a series of deep, controlled breaths. "I needed a mother desperately, but she wasn't able to be one."

Deep breaths: in for four, out for seven.

The words hurt me more than I realised, and I knew that the hurt was written on my face, embedded within the weak tone of my voice when I spoke.

She handed me a tissue, as tears began to form in my eyes. Great; the session had barely begun, and I had already turned on the water-works. But Victoria didn't seem to mind. In fact, I guess she was accustomed to my ups and downs by now.

"And your father? What kind of man was he?"

"My *father*… he had a tendency to be quite violent, and he was a deeply pessimistic man. I grew up in fear at the prospect of his arrival home from work each day. I often hid away in my bedroom; the moment his car pulled up in the drive, I disappeared."

I swallowed hard, and my throat, I realised, felt considerably dry and sore. Reaching into my bag, which was propped at the side of my chair, I extracted a bottle of water, though not 'Evian' like Victoria Green's. I never understood why Evian water was always more expensive than the others, such as Nestle, Buxton, and Volvic. In fact, what were all these brands of water that ironically all had the same taste?

One small sip, followed by two larger gulps, and I put the lid back on the bottle, resting it on the table by the glass vase; this time, it was filled with a cluster of purple and white flowers that I didn't know the name of. They were beautiful, nonetheless.

Victoria nodded, encouraging me to say more, though I had nothing more to add without her asking me further questions. I needed her to lead the conversation, for it was almost as if I had no backbone any more. However, strangely, I felt it easier to talk about my father than I did my mother, as I realised there and then that her absence had caused me the most pain. What could be more tragic than a child who needs her mother, and even though her mother is there physically, she is never able to be more than that? My mother couldn't show love; she was weak, and could not protect her children the way a mother is supposed to. She could not protect me from the things I was afraid of; she couldn't protect me from my father, nor the bullies, nor the many traumas that lay ahead.

"What was it that you were afraid of?" asked Victoria softly, broaching the subject with caution and fragility.

"I was scared of *him*... my father... my grandfather and the man that lived next door,"

A silence lingered between Victoria and I, and I realised that it was a comfortable silence, despite the topic of conversation. In fact, that silence provided me with just enough time to realise that I was safe here in her company.

"Why were you afraid of those men? Did it stem from your fathers' violence?" she asked, after a moment. "Did things occur between yourself and the other men?"

I don't know why, but Victoria Green's questions seemed to bring me to full consciousness, and wake me from all the inner diversions I had created from ever having to think about certain events and face them full on. Sadly, my sense of safety was brief, for with these questions came a raw fear that I needed a moment to make sense of, before I could even answer.

How is it that words, phrases, and questions can make us feel so afraid?

The mind is such a powerful thing, and to actually understand it takes a lifetime of practice. I wondered if Victoria completely understood her own mind, and whether she was really at peace with everything; I knew I would never know the answer to that question. My mind somehow felt like the most complicated one of all, and almost like it was a time bomb that could go off at any moment; even I couldn't predict when that might be.

"I was afraid of him because of his violence. I was afraid of them because..." I couldn't finish the sentence; my words were lost inside of me, and my speech had become slow and unsteady.

"It's okay," urged Victoria. "You don't need to be afraid in here, in this room; this is a safe place. Are you afraid of me?"

"No." I shook my head.

"Do you feel safe here?"

"Yes," I replied, and engaged in several deep breaths, which brought with them the heavy flow of tears that had been waiting patiently for permission to fall.

I felt safe in the room in which we sat, and I felt safe in her company, though I did not feel safe within myself. She offered me another tissue and I thanked her, wiping my cheeks, which had become stained so quickly. It felt safe to cry here.

"I can't pinpoint the exact thing which made me afraid... it's more a series of small things that I think of. And yet they don't seem to be 'enough' for such a huge fear." As I spoke, I felt I was trying to figure myself out, trying to remember something; it seemed there was a missing piece to the jigsaw puzzle. I think she sensed this.

"The brain is an extremely complex organ, and it works in strange ways, sometimes suppressing certain events. So you mustn't worry about it – we will figure this out."

"When? When will I figure this out? When am I going to be okay again?"

"It's going to take time; it will be a long process, and, believe me, if I could wave a magic wand and make everything okay in this instant, I would."

Though I believed her, this phrase felt a little too cliché for my liking, so I did not respond to it directly. Instead, I continued my tragic journey down memory lane, silently at first, but then I felt able to share my recollections with her once again.

"I remember... being adopted by a nice family was my wish, every birthday when I blew out the candles on my cake. But, as the number of candles increased, I knew the chance of my wish coming true was becoming less and less."

I took another deep breath. I didn't even know how I was managing to say these words to her, but they just flowed right off my tongue, like a drop of wax running down one of those coloured birthday candles.

"Would you say you had a lonely childhood?" asked Victoria.

She sat back on her chair, legs crossed, still giving me her full and undivided attention. Her face expressed just the right amount of sympathy, mixed with a hint of compassion and understanding, yet, at the same time, it wasn't too much. I felt myself really starting to warm to her today, for nobody had ever focused on me as much as she was doing throughout these sessions; nobody had ever tried to get to the root of my issues before, and I had always needed that, whether I was aware of it or not.

"Yes," I said, with that familiar quiver in my voice. "I needed parents growing up; doesn't every child? I was bullied at school too, and, when three o'clock arrived and the school day had come to an end, I would only return to another place of bullying."

She nodded her head, showing me she understood what I had gone through, and how difficult it was.

"That must have felt incredibly lonely."

"Yes." I nodded, gazing absent-mindedly at the purple and white flowers on the table. "I remember the first time I got hurt, physically, by a group of older girls, on my way home through the park. They cornered me, pushed me down to the ground, and kicked me repeatedly. It wasn't that the unremitting blows hurt me. No, I don't remember any physical pain at all. I just remember the heavy loneliness that had wrapped itself around me that day."

"That must have been very distressing," she said, softly uncrossing her legs now, as though she was making herself more comfortable, in order to make me in return feel more at ease… and I did. "How did you deal with that?"

"Well, I often shut myself away in my room, and, as I told you before, I was self-harming. I can't be sure, but I think maybe my bulimia started around that time too."

"How old were you when you first self-harmed?"

"Eleven. I cut my wrists with the sharp edge of a ruler; it was nothing excessive, 'superficial wounds', they called them. I think I was crying out for help, as I let people at school see the marks; I didn't attempt to hide them. And I remember one of the teachers was so nice

128

with me, but then she told my mother... I guess because I was so young."

More tears ran down my cheeks and fell onto my trousers, leaving tiny stains that I knew would soon dry up again, leaving no trace of this conversation. Victoria watched me as I cried; she looked sad for me.

"What did your mother do?"

"She was angry. She screamed at me for causing her embarrassment, and then..." I paused for a moment; "...she told me to wear long-sleeves so my father wouldn't know. And life went on as though nothing had ever happened."

"Why do you think she didn't want your father to know?"

"I don't know... shame? Fear, perhaps? I'm really not sure. I remember everyone seemed to be scared of him: my mother, me, my sister."

"Why do you think your sister was afraid of him?"

I paused for a long moment, as painful images of her being beaten, abused, and humiliated completely took over my mind.

"He hurt her. I was scared of him because I saw what he did to her. And I was always aware that I might be next. At nighttime, I slept with a wooden wedge pushed under my door, so nobody from the outside could enter."

Victoria rubbed her chin thoughtfully with her thumb and forefinger, then she crossed her legs, sat back on the chair, and said: "This all sounds very distressing for you; you were only a child, and shouldn't have had to go through that." She shook her head. "You had similar fears about Mohamed when you were in Egypt, am I right?"

"Yes."

"Do you think they may have sprouted from those fears you had of your father and of the other male figures in your life?"

"Yes I do. That would make a lot of sense actually."

"Can you remember a particular incident with Mohamed that made you feel so afraid?"

The answer again was 'yes', though the question alone caused the tiny hairs on my arms to stand on end, as one memory after the next resurfaced. One particular evening, when Mohamed, Leila, and I were lying in bed together ready to sleep, Leila got up to go to the bathroom, leaving he and I alone in bed. Her absence. His presence. I immediately felt tense and nervous... then he touched my stomach with the tips of his fingers, running them up and down my bare skin. I pretended to be sleeping, all the while praying for Leila to return. Mohamed moved closer, and began to touch me in more intimate places. Then, to my relief, Leila returned. I thought he would stop... he didn't. Instead, Leila joined in. I pretended to wake just at that moment, and then left the bed, went to the bathroom... I sat on the floor, and cried into a towel to minimise the noise.

I told this to Victoria in a voice that was quiet and unsteady; she looked truly saddened and affected by my words. This only emphasised what I already knew: that she was the right person for me to confide in, and that I needn't worry or be angry with her, or even feel patronised by her. Victoria Green was here to help me, and I needed to work with her.

Chapter Ten

Cairo, December 2014

I sat up in the large bed we shared, still entwined within the white, cotton sheets. I watched her as she packed her bag hurriedly, throwing in a couple of short-sleeved tops, her laptop, and several pairs of underwear. She moved around the room swiftly, as though she was nervous about something; it was almost as if her mood mirrored my own feeling of anxiety. Once again, we were on the same level, thinking about the same things, yet in very different ways. She barely made eye contact with me, for she knew what was on my mind. She knew my worries, and then... I just couldn't hold the question inside me a moment longer, for fear of it burning a hole in my chest.

"Is Mohamed going to come while you are with your family?" I asked Leila nervously, unsure of whether my asking this question was going to cause a conflict I couldn't handle.

She shot me a sharp look, as though she had in fact been waiting for me to dare to ask her this question, and then she turned away quickly, as though she might be able to avoid the depth of this conversation if she appeared busy enough. After throwing an additional two items into her bag, Leila stopped what she was doing.

"Yes, probably. It's his house too, Abi!" she replied finally. Her tone was abrupt, which made me feel all the more afraid.

Though she was right – it *was* his house too – he didn't spend all his time in it, for he still half-lived with his mother and sister, in a much bigger house opposite Abdin Palace. But I was always aware that he could arrive at any given moment: morning, afternoon, or night, I never knew. It was around 10.30 a.m., and incredibly cool in the house, causing the hairs on my arms to stand on end, though this may have also been a result of the fear that loomed over me. I often felt cold when I was afraid, or even unwell.

"What will I do?" I asked her fearfully, waiting and hoping for her to feel me, and understand the worries I was holding inside.

It was as though suddenly I had transformed into a small child, and I was asking my mother for help, quietly hoping she wouldn't leave me behind with the *monster*. I was suddenly aware of just how dependent I had become on her, and I detested this part of myself; I felt disgusted in my behaviour, yet unable to do anything about it.

"Oh, Abi... just like normal, whatever you want." She zipped up her rucksack, which signified a closure to the conversation, and I was aware that my time was almost up.

The clock was ticking loudly in the background, though the sound of my heart beating rapidly somehow drowned out this noise.

I could see her becoming impatient with me, and, in all fairness, I shouldn't have kept pushing her, but I was also becoming increasingly nervous of what might be around the corner for me. I knew he would try to touch me, kiss me; the moment she left, I knew he would want to come to me. He was always trying to be alone with me, but, so far, I had always found excuses. I had, in some way, been lucky up until now.

"Leila, I'm nervous. I don't want to stay alone with him." I blurted the words out, seeing it as my last chance.

"ABI!"

She must have known how I felt about this, even before I had voiced it so directly. She was my best friend, my closest companion – we knew everything about each other – but I think she just chose to avoid some things, choosing to free herself of the responsibility. I hated this about her – the way she drained life of all the good things, all the things she liked and wanted, but left the results and consequences to deal with themselves.

"He's YOUR boyfriend! Why do I have to stay with him?" I shouted at her, feeling more and more anxious, and angry with her for not listening – for not hearing my cry for help.

Another wave of desperation swept over me.

She stepped towards me, and, simultaneously, I shielded myself with my arms, as though protecting my face from the hurt I suspected was coming my way – though no physical attack came.

"He's yours too, remember?" she replied, in a tone that held some darkness I hadn't witnessed in her before.

She has uttered these same words on numerous occasions, reminding me of the twisted situation in which we lived.

"Leila, I'm just not comfortable with being alone with him, without you. Not yet. Please."

Fear, dread, and desperation rang out in my voice as I spoke. I never felt comfortable with Mohamed, but when Leila was there, at least I could relax and feel a little safe to some extent as the pressure 'to entertain him' was not on me alone. I moved from the bed and started to put on some clothes that were laid out on the chair at the end of the room; I moved fast, as though he might come at any moment.

"Abi, you want me to tell him not to come to *his* house or what? Be direct!"

"I don't know. I just don't want to stay alone with him; he's still a stranger to me, and he makes me uncomfortable."

"FUCK! Abi, I can't do this every time! Every time you need me, and don't want to stay alone. You say I am crazy when I fight with you? Look at *you*!"

The harshness of her words stung my ears, and settled inside of me like a cancerous tumour – one that needs removing fast before it spreads and the real chaos begins. Poor Leila was always labelled the 'crazy one' because of her anger, her crazy outbursts of rage, and her lack of control. But I knew she had a point about me. I was filled with both anger and hurt as her words still clung to me, clawing at me, telling me I was weak.

'Why won't she help me?' I asked myself, again and again.

Should I *want* to stay with him?

"Do you think I like myself like this?" I began, softly, with tears forming in my eyes. "I am fully aware of *my* faults, and I go to sleep every night wishing to be different; I wish I was okay. I wish I had a loving family, a stable background, and a stable character. But I DON'T. I don't have that. And it's not my fault; surely I am punished enough by my own mind and character, without you waltzing in to tell me how crazy I am... because believe me, I KNOW! There isn't a day that passes by when I don't feel the full, intensified weight of my pathetic, hopeless character. But, after what I grew up with, it would be an absolute miracle if I didn't have some kind of psychological disorder – A FUCKING MIRACLE!" I spat the words out at her, with every ounce of emotion I was feeling, and, even though I knew she wouldn't understand many of the complex words I had just used, I didn't offer her any translation.

Right now, my face and tone of voice said it all. I started to cry – a little at first, but then uncontrollably. The tears and wails seeped out of me, as though I had held the world on my shoulders for far too long.

Leila was silent and distant for a moment; perhaps she was considering what she should do, or maybe she was shocked at my sudden outburst. But then, the warmer part of her made an appearance, just before it really was too late.

"Abi.... I'm sorry. Come here." She was suddenly calmer now, as she wrapped her arms around me. "I will call him and ask what he will do in these days."

I continued to cry, though my wailing softened, until it was merely heavy breathing, followed by inconsistent sniffles.

I think, in that moment, Leila saw how much I had pushed myself to accept this situation, and I think she saw sense to help her friend. Or perhaps she just felt sorry to see me cry. We hugged for a while, and then she told me in a quiet and more casual voice that she would go to the other room to make a call. I knew it was to Mohamed without her confirming this, and, though I felt slightly more at ease by her doing so, there was also a part of me fearing his reaction. She left me, and I waited. I strained my ears to listen, but then quickly decided I did not wish to hear, so I searched for diversion.

Rummaging through my desk drawer, I extracted my box of cigarettes, and stepped out onto the balcony to smoke. I was wearing shorts and a strap-top, so I was wary before peering down onto the street below. There was the man again, in his grey robe, washing a car, and further up from him were several middle-aged men, sat on stools, drinking tea from glass cups. My eyes searched the street for stray cats, and I immediately spotted several scavenging beneath cars, their fur matted and covered in dust, just like everything else. I inhaled deeply and exhaled, taking a tiny amount of pleasure from my cigarette, which was all I could find to make me feel relaxed, if only for a moment. I stood there for around fifteen minutes, people -watching, and smoking cigarette after cigarette, until I felt a wave of dizziness pass over me from inhaling too much nicotine.

Soft footsteps approached me from behind.

"He's not coming," she said quietly, opening the door that led out onto the balcony.

"Okay," I replied softly, relieved, yet I knew from her voice, and the length of their call, that Mohamed had given her a hard time.

"What will you do today?" she asked me, offering a much-needed diversion.

"Walk for little, watch TV maybe…" I paused, and then added: "I love you."

"I love you too."

"I'm sorry."

"Me too."

Chapter Eleven

London, April 2015

Opening the Tesco bag, I extracted a chocolate cake, a bag of cheese-flavoured Doritos, a king-size Mars Bar, a chicken tikka wrap, and a vanilla milkshake. Within those thirty seconds, the atmosphere in my bedroom was filled with a rustle of packets, mixed with the lighter rustle of the carrier bag. I started with the cake. With shaking hands, I tore open the cardboard box, ripped off the cellophane, and dug a spoon into the perfectly formed cake. It cut through the first layer of icing, the sponge, cream, and then more sponge. I scooped up a large chunk, balancing it on the spoon until it reached my mouth. It tasted so good. I repeated the action again and again, until my face was covered in chocolate and I had devoured half of the chocolate cake. Next, I began working my way through the chicken tikka wrap, which gave me further satisfaction. Then, I took two large bites from the Mars Bar, before returning to the chocolate cake. My stomach was beginning to feel swollen, and the familiar feeling of sickness was slowly creeping up on me. This only made me try to work my way through the pile of food even faster, until all that was left were the mere crumbs from each item I had purchased that night. I felt very sick. Looking at the massacre of packets, boxes, and bags on my carpet, I felt utterly disgusted in myself and what I had just done. Though I had not finished – the next step awaited. Quickly, I ran to the bathroom, put my fingers to the back of my throat as far as I could, and pressed down. Pushing on my stomach with my other hand encouraged the vomit to come out: once, twice, brown-coloured vomit escaped me; the third time brought up some pieces of lettuce from the chicken tikka wrap. And finally, the fourth time, which was more chocolate cake, I could take it no more. My stomach still felt full, though not of food, but of the action itself. I drank some water from the tap, after swirling several mouthfuls and washing my face. Exhausted, I returned to my room and lay on my back. Moments later, I went to the bathroom again and tried to purge one more time, but I couldn't, and this made me angry. I drank some more water, and then I slept.

***

"I'm still scared."

These were the first words to come out of my mouth that morning, when I sat down on the chair across from her. "Even though my situation is different, I still have the same fears inside of me, and I don't understand why. Some days I'm too afraid to go outside, and, if somebody knocks on the door, I become frightened, fearful of... I don't know what of exactly. But I'm just... incredibly anxious *all the time*."

It was 10:15 a.m., and I was her first client. She was the first person whom I had broken words with since waking up, yet they rolled off my tongue like a flock of caged birds being granted freedom into the vast open sky. My stomach still felt slightly swollen and tender from last night's binge-eating episode, and I knew today I must consume very little to make up for it. In fact, I'd started by skipping breakfast completely. Helen had left for work at around 7.30 a.m., so I had had to promise her the night before that I would attend, despite her absence. That was right before I had devoured the cake, the chocolate, and the chicken tikka wrap.

I couldn't behave like a child forever; I had to take responsibility for my own life, and I certainly could not be accompanied by my sister everywhere. Now I had been meeting Victoria for four months; some mornings I absolutely dreaded seeing her; other mornings I ran to those meetings, looking forward to the prospect of sharing my feelings with her, and hopefully receiving some condolence. But today, I was filled with an overwhelming fear. I couldn't even explain it, I just woke up that way. I woke up, and I feared everything around me; I cursed my very existence, and I hated the fact that I couldn't just walk into the next room and find Leila sitting there with a cup of tea in her hand, that familiar smile on her face, and just her overall presence. I missed her so much; why wasn't it getting any easier?

It was one of those mornings where I needed her hugs. I needed to laugh and smile with her, but we were countries apart, and that space between England and Egypt was about the same size as the hole in my heart.

I couldn't bear it any longer.

"Are you afraid of Mohamed?" asked Victoria, sitting up in her chair and taking a drink from her coffee; it was in one of those cardboard takeaway cups, which I instantly recognised from the café just outside. "Or perhaps you are afraid of your father?"

We looked at each other, and I didn't know which one of those made me the most uncomfortable: Mohamed or my father?

I knew, however, that both of those names brought with them an abundant amount of fear, discomfort, and a sickening sensation that rested in the pit of my stomach.

"Yes, I am," I said quietly. "Even though I know they are both far away, sometimes I just have the fear inside me, with no cause, no trigger. It just arrives from nowhere. Yes, it's the same fear I often felt with either my father or Mohamed, but with no image, no thought of him. Does that make any sense?" I looked at her with a sense of doubt, as I knew how odd my words must seem; *I* couldn't even make sense of them. "I'm afraid of myself."

I looked at her for what seemed like forever, questioningly, as though asking her: 'what does it mean and why am I like this?'

I felt nervous, even in the moment I waited for her reply, as though I might not even be able to handle *that*.

"Remember, Abi, when we spoke about Post-Traumatic Stress? Well, this is part of it. Sometimes the feeling remains, and it can be hard to let go of; sometimes you may find there is a trigger in the present that will arouse a familiar feeling from the past, such as fear; and sometimes there may be no trigger at all. Just know that I am here to help you through this difficult time – I'm not going to leave you." She smiled slightly, and I felt reassured. "Mental Health is a very complex field, with many roads and alleys leading in numerous directions. I will help solve your problems in time. This you can be sure of; I am not going to abandon you."

I looked at her for a moment, and responded to her smile. I liked her words, and took great comfort from them. My eyes resumed staring at the laminate floor beneath my feet, and a beige-patterned rug with intricate details I'd never noticed before. It was placed partially beneath the wooden table, leaving only around half of it visible, though still it surprised me that I hadn't noticed it before today. Yet I was strangely aware that it had always been there. Making eye-contact had never been an easy thing for me, and, during conversations, I often looked anywhere but at the person speaking to me, focusing on nearby objects, or gazing out of the window until my mind was lost in thought. I thought I had memorised every detail of that room by now, whilst conjuring up scenes of Egypt – some imaginary, others memories.

"It feels like it was only yesterday. The pain I have, the heartache, and loss – it's as though everything happened only yesterday," I said, aware that my voice was coming across sleepy, hypnotic even, as I started to lose sense of reality.

I felt so detached from my body that I couldn't be sure where I was anymore.

Victoria began to appear blurry, until her entire body seemed to merge into the chair she was sat on, which in turn began to merge into the wall behind it.

Looking downwards slightly now, my eyes rested on a shiny, black surface, which at first was hazy, moving almost, like black tar slowly running down a slope under a hot sun. However, as the black tar swam into focus, and familiar shapes began to form, I could see they were in fact the black, patent-shoes I was wearing. Far away thoughts began to invade the present once more. They had been a gift from Mohamed – the black, patent-shoes – around three weeks before I'd left. I believe he was trying to win my heart; he had obviously begun to understand that my love for Leila would never waver, whereas my love for him barely existed beyond the four-letter word itself. He knew that, yet he never gave up on me, and often came to me with kind gestures, and beautiful gifts such as *these shoes*. The centre of Cairo was filled with shoe shops, and most of the shoes I currently owned had come from one of those many outlets, crammed together on Sherif Street, Talaat Harb Street, and 26th July Street. It was as though anybody opening a shop in Cairo felt they had to sell shoes, or sunglasses – another popular item amongst the dusty, cobbled streets, chipped and cracked like the wrinkled faces of old men sitting on wooden stools in the rare and sacred patches of shade. The centre was extremely famous for its sunglasses, though far more than necessary of those shops existed too. They weren't even spaced out accordingly; there were literally around four or five shops specialising in sunglasses on one street, and two right next-door to each other. As I began to picture the centre of Cairo in my mind, and the golden shimmer of its evening sunset shimmied into focus like the rear of a belly dancer, I was suddenly transported to one particular occasion when he had taken Leila and I to Etoile, a famous dessert shop with a small yet well-furnished café upstairs. We had sat together amongst normal Egyptian couples on leisurely outings, laughing and smiling as though there were no problems in the secluded and bizarre world we usually lived in. I had ordered cherry cheesecake, Mohamed had ordered cream caramel, and Leila had opted for her own favourite too: white cream cake. Etoile was our favourite dessert shop; we adored choosing from the vast rows of fancy cakes displayed in a large glass cabinet. Even though Mohamed did not favour the sweeter foods, he always bought them for Leila and I, and then sometimes, like that day, he would come and share the experience with us, watching with satisfaction as both of his women smiled and laughed together.

"Mmm, this must be what heaven tastes like," I said, as I placed a delicate forkful of cherry cheesecake into my mouth. "It's amazing!"

Mohamed watched me as I licked the fork clean with my tongue; his expression was cheeky and lustful. I knew what was on his mind. I ignored it, and continued to enjoy my cake, though in a more subtle manner.

"Wow," said Leila, licking the white frosting from her own fork. "How's yours, Mohamed?"

He looked away from me, and smiled at Leila, who looked so exquisitely beautiful and sumptuous when she ate. And so happy, too, yet seemingly oblivious to the abnormality of our situation.

She seemed to live in a rare, deluded world, where all of these things that didn't make sense in our lives were actually considered normal within her rather obscure mindset. Leila puzzled me greatly, and I knew that something wasn't quite right about her – the way she could lose control of her anger, the way she accepted the abnormal as... well, normal, and the way in which she was quite promiscuous, unlike any other woman I had come across. Mental illness was not really recognised throughout Egypt, and therefore there were no such tests available to diagnose anybody. There were no treatments either; in fact, the people who did have some kind of disorder or abnormality were usually hidden away, cast out onto the streets, or paraded throughout the city in order to obtain money through begging. Whatever was wrong with Leila was nowhere near as extreme as this, yet, having spent a considerable amount of time living within such close proximity to her, it became evident to me that, had we been in England, there would have been help available for Leila. However, we were in the centre of Cairo, living in a situation that aggravated and tore at our minds, bodies and… would it be too extreme to say 'souls' too?

"Good," he said, smiling at our happy faces. "Very good."

It seemed he felt pleased he had put the smiles on our faces. His work was done – he had been the dutiful boyfriend for an hour. Mohamed, I believe, was not oblivious to the abnormality of our situation, yet he played his cards well; he made the right moves, and he did his best to make me feel as equal a part for him as Leila. He made sure he took what he wanted, of course, despite the damage it was doing, yet there was his good side too, always lingering close by.

"Hey, let's take a photo," said Leila, reaching into her brown leather bag for her phone.

Her eyes lit up; it was obvious she was excited, and wanted to record something that I could only imagine was a highlighted moment in her life.

"Okay," I said, cleaning the remainder of the red sauce from my fork, and reluctantly budging closer to Mohamed. I didn't even make eye-contact with him.

I just focused on the camera, and the picture about to be captured of us, always aware of his presence, uncomfortable about it, yet cleverly disguising it.

Leila was sat on the other side of Mohamed now, so he was in the middle, just how he liked it. She set the phone camera to take the photo in ten seconds. I put on my best smile, and so did they.

We all appeared in the highest of spirits together; it was for the briefest of moments, but the photographic evidence produced would represent something different for each of us.

I kept that photo; I have it today, attached to the wall in my room in London.

"Abi?" Victoria's voice brought me back.

"What?" I replied, as though I had been paying attention, but her smile made me blush, and I apologised for my brief absence. "I was just… thinking."

She appeared concerned; I could see from the look in her eyes, and the way she tilted her head thoughtfully, watching me all the while.

"What were you thinking about?" she asked me gently.

"Egypt… Mohamed… Leila."

I told her about the scene I had just remembered, and she asked me: "There were some happy times between the three of you, weren't there?"

"There were some *bearable* times between the three of us," I corrected, with a light smile, and a shake of my head at the memory and thoughts my own words had brought. "I suppose there were some happier times," I added, as the ache in my heart slowly caught up with me; it was filled with the loss of something.

The questions from Victoria passed by quicker than usual that day, and my anxiety had lessened a notch or two. In fact, before I knew it, the session was over, and I was on my way home, walking through the cool, late-morning air. I wrapped my black coat tighter around my body, fastening it in a double-knot with the belt attached, and clutched the ends of my grey woollen scarf to prevent them blowing in the wind, as I moved at a steady pace, using all my senses to appreciate the scene that surrounded me. The bright, blue sky, the sun that kept on creeping from behind a mass of white clouds, and the soft touch of the breeze on my skin, fresh and energising, as if it was feeding me with a power that earlier I had not possessed. A middle-aged man in a grey, pin-striped suit and an elegantly dressed woman with highlights in her hair passed by me; they were holding hands, and appeared to be engrossed in pleasant conversation – a normal married couple. Across the narrow street, there was a woman with her two children following her, waddling like two little ducks on the embankment; the woman was wearing loose clothing and a scarf over her head, covering her hair. She was a Muslim. I liked that about London – how it had become less and less English, and more and more multi-cultural. It wasn't so strange to see an Indian or Chinese person walking down the street, or a Muslim. When I was in Egypt, I was always being stared at for my pale skin and mass of light-brown hair, chaotic, curly, and much softer than theirs. I was told that, several years ago, Egypt used to have a vast amount of tourism, but, due to all the political problems with President Morsi and the Muslim-Brotherhood, the streets were often full of danger – terrorist attacks and violent protests. The foreigners became less and less, as the media portrayed the country to be violated, corrupt, and dangerous. I must have looked back several times at the Muslim lady, for it was a 'connection' to my recent past that I just couldn't let go of. I looked back again and again, until eventually she disappeared around a bend in the road, and I was left only with the memory of her. 'How peculiar,' I thought to myself, 'that something I associated only with Egypt was within such a short distance from me just moments ago.'

Life has a way of surprising us, keeping us on the edge of our seats, curious, wondering what will happen next and why… why all of this?

I arrived at the door of my sister's apartment, and let myself in with the key I had had for several years now, though this was the most I had ever used it.

"Hi!" I chirped, in a voice that was much more upbeat than the usual one, which was heavily burdened with my pain.

"Hi. How did it go today?" asked Helen. "It was just a half day for me today – everyone's breaking up for half-term, hence my being back so early."

She was sat on the couch with her feet up, browsing idly through a pile of papers, still dressed in her work attire, though she'd removed her jacket.

It seemed strange to see her in this relaxed mood, yet it suited her, and it made me feel somewhat more relaxed too.

"It was okay. Do you fancy having some lunch? Maybe we could go outside and do something different today," I suggested casually.

"Hmm… okay. You're in a pleasant mood – should I be worried?" asked Helen, putting down the paperwork and turning to face me.

I noticed she had the vanilla-scented Yankee candle lit.

"Not at all. I'm just… trying, I guess." I smiled, sitting down next to her, inhaling the divine scent.

"Well, that seems optimistic. I suppose we should go and have some lunch then." And with that, she stood up and began to put on her jacket that lay just beside her; it was a black, pin-striped jacket, and the moment she put it on, she suddenly appeared professional and elegant once again.

She leant over the table and blew out the candle, leaving behind a delicate spiral of smoke that rose higher and higher until disappearing into the air.

I smiled and handed her the beige handbag she took everywhere; it was resting on the table, with her pile of papers from work that she had so graciously put aside, and, within less than a minute, we were on our way outside to have lunch.

"Why don't we go to Manchow Wok – you know, the Chinese takeaway just down the street?" she suggested. "They serve the best shrimp and noodles, and they have those little white takeaway boxes you like so much." She laughed, shaking her head at me.

It was true; I had loved those little white boxes ever since I had seen them in movies – movies I had watched with Leila. Leila and I watched a lot of movies together, for Mohamed always downloaded them for us – all the newly released ones too – and, whenever we saw the characters eating together, they always seemed to be eating Chinese takeaway. She too used to comment on this. On the days when we had enough money, we would go to eat Chinese; it was her favourite, ever since she had worked in a Chinese restaurant long before she had met me. There was a shopping mall in Cairo called Carrefour, located in a beautiful, upper-class district called Maadi, and, when Mohamed gave us some money to go out and have fun, we would travel by microbus to Carrefour and go to the Chinese restaurant, Zen. We would always go in the evening, as it was open until eleven, and, during daylight, the sun was unbearable for taking public transport. We would get dressed up, standing together in the oval-shaped mirror to apply make-up – thick, black eyeliner and mascara – and then off we would go to wait in the street for the microbus that went to Maadi. Those microbuses in Cairo were tiny little vehicles, holding only around seven passengers in total, so when it arrived, me, Leila, and five other Egyptian passengers would cram together in the two rows of seats in the back, as we were thrown from left to right to centre throughout the journey. Due to Cairo's broken roads, the bus would jump and jerk over every crack, rock, and dip in the street, and the journey itself always brought so much laughter, as we tried not to have any physical contact with the person sat next to us (which was nearly impossible each time the driver stopped abruptly or swerved unexpectedly.) I remember watching the liveliness of the street from the window, which was always open to allow some air inside, so we could breathe amidst the heat; malnourished children with scrawny hair and dirty clothes would tap on car windows, asking for spare change; older men would walk up and down selling bread shaped like large pretzels, and the glitter of lights from shops sparkled as we passed. However, the most exciting part was always when we spotted the large, white mall with illuminated, blue writing, which read "Carrefour." Leila would take me by the hand and lead me out onto the sandy road, which we would run across, kicking up dust and dirt, so we could quickly get to the mall and be part of something that, at the time, was incredibly exciting for us.

Inside was such a contrast to Cairo itself, to the Cairo where we lived, in which poverty loomed in every direction. There was none of that inside Carrefour. It was like a shopping mall in England: shiny, artificial, illuminated. Everything sparkled and glittered, like a sea of jewels in every colour, shape, and size. Even for me, having been brought up in England, this still excited me, for I had been deprived of it for so long.

"Where shall we go first?" I would ask her, slipping my arm through hers.

I always asked her questions like this, for she was the leader, the mother figure, and I was her child.

Usually we would browse the clothes shops first, picking up items we could never afford, yet enjoying the visual luxury they provided; being there always made us feel rich and more civilised than it often seemed we were within the walls of our apartment. Afterwards, we would automatically make our way across the shiny, white flooring, which was so iridescent and sanitised due to the laborious work of the cleaning attendants, and then straight towards the Chinese restaurant. Each time, we would order a large variety of things, though our favourite was the shrimp with noodles.

"So, what are you ordering?" asked Helen, as we browsed the menu that was fixed to the wall inside. "I think I will get steamed rice and the sweet and sour chicken."

I didn't need to look at the menu.

"I will have the shrimp with noodles." I smiled. "I'll get them."

"Are you sure?" she asked, always aware that I usually needed looking after, and was often struggling financially.

"Yes." I smiled again. "Go sit down, I'll bring it when it's ready."

Our afternoon was a pleasurable one, consisting of delicious food, filled with exotic memories, mixed with a leisurely stroll in and out of shops just like the ones in Carrefour. We engaged in idle chatter, then had a Costa break, where we ordered one of our few shared pleasures: cappuccino and a slice of carrot cake. An additional bonus to the day was that the weather had remained bright and pleasant, with barely a cloud in sight, though the air still held a harsh coolness to it that I felt each time we stopped. We must have been outside the house for around three hours in total, which was the most I had achieved since being back in London. It was a delightful change; *I* was a delightful change. Within those glorious hours, there was no sign whatsoever of the young woman who suffered from depression, anxiety, and hid beneath the duvet cover, cowering away from the demands *and* pleasures of life; she had decided to stay away during those hours. When we did return, however, I realised I had left my phone behind on the large double-bed I slept in, and immediately noticed it flashing with missed calls. I knew it could only be one person, and, just as I was beginning to browse through them, she called again.

"Hello," I said with a smile. "How are you?"

There was a silence from the other end, and then I heard that she was crying.

"I miss you, Abi. I miss you so much."

I paused, for I knew her feeling, but didn't know what I could say to make her okay.

"Please come back, Abi."

"Leila... I..."

"Please, Abi."

Chapter Twelve

Cairo, January 2015

The day I stepped onto that plane and left Leila in Cairo was one of the most excruciating blows my heart had ever experienced. I felt like death had paid a visit into my life, and taken away everybody I had ever cared about. Because that's what Leila was to me; she was my mother, my sister, and my best friend, all combined within one beautiful person. I felt my soul had been ripped from my body in such a brutal way that I didn't think life could ever stand a chance of being wholesome and meaningful again. I had to come to terms with it. But, the thing was, I didn't; I couldn't. I couldn't accept it. No matter how hard I tried, and no matter how many diversions I created, there was always that emptiness that lingered inside of me from the moment I said 'goodbye'. Each morning, I spoke to Victoria Green about my feelings, and every walk I took through the streets of London, I carried with me that heavy feeling of pure emptiness, and wondered incessantly, over and over, how the feeling of emptiness could in fact be so *heavy*.

"I love you, Leila," I whispered to her, as I lay in the bed next to her, sobbing quietly.

It was 2:30 a.m. and I couldn't sleep, knowing that tomorrow we would go to the airport and say our final goodbyes. It just didn't seem real, or even right for that matter. Leila and I were the same; we were part of each other, and, separated, we would never stand a chance of survival in this brutal world. I knew this – I was sure of it – but the last clash had ended with Mohamed stating that he had had enough of all the fighting. He had been so angry that day, and told us both to leave. The thing was, we could no longer survive financially just Leila and I. Not to mention the manipulative hold Mohamed had over her, which resulted in her not being able to stay with me if he wasn't present. I had booked a flight using almost all my savings. Leila had accompanied me to the travel agents', and acted as a translator, trying to find the best offer. And that was that. It was a one-way, non-refundable flight ticket from Cairo to London. Just hours later, however, we were filled with regret, and Mohamed was even angrier than before, telling Leila over the phone how stupid and childish we both were. He refused to even visit us after that day. I was relieved with this outcome.

"Come here," she said, moving closer to me beneath the white sheet we were sharing, just the two of us. "I love you too. I'm going to miss you so much, Habibi."

She hugged me tight and, as she did so, I could feel the whole world slipping through my fingers; it suddenly seemed too frail to grasp onto even the tiniest molecule of hope.

How could it be over?

We had travelled to hell and back together – surely this meant we could survive anything. Surely we were destined to stay together. Her hugs had always brought me great comfort; they had always made me feel relaxed and complete, but not this time. This time, all I could feel was the sense of losing something that shouldn't be lost, and it was all happening so slowly; it was pure torture. It felt

153

very wrong, cruel, unfair. I had already put myself through hell to stay with her; I had slept with Mohamed, and each time he came to me it felt like rape. It hurt me – it destroyed me – and I did it all to stay with Leila, because she filled that giant, gaping hole in my life.

"I can't imagine sleeping alone after all this time with you." I cried harder into her arms, soaking her t-shirt with my tears.

"We will meet again… let's just think of this as a vacation apart."

"Insh'allah," I replied, which was Arabic for 'if God wants it to be.' Egyptians were always saying 'Insh'allah' to almost every question, yet I did not appreciate the uncertainty of its meaning. "I love you so much," I added in a whisper.

"I love you too," she whispered back in my ear, so close that her words tickled me, though I didn't smile; instead, I lay there and listened to Leila as she started to cry too.

That night I only got around four hours' sleep, but we still woke early to finish packing and spend the last moments together. Leila would leave the apartment and go to her parents' house, and, of course, I would be going to London to stay with my sister, although I had not yet informed her of my arrival. I guess I had been hoping for some miracle that would allow me to stay, but it never came. Looking around, the room in which we had spent all our time together, making memory after memory, suddenly appeared so bare, as most of our possessions had been packed away. In fact, the place looked much larger than it had seemed during that time. I closed my suitcase, securing all its contents inside, and the sound of the zip closing echoed until, before I knew it, Leila and I were travelling to the airport together in a taxi, tightly holding hands throughout the tense journey, praying for the car to drive slower, or perhaps never even reach the airport.

Sadly, after thirty painfully silent minutes, the taxi pulled up at the airport terminal and we got out. Leila took my suitcase, whilst I paid the driver.

"Shok'ran," I said to him, as a light breeze blew through my curly hair, sending it into a wild dance. It was the only part of me that possessed any life as I watched the world around me pass by.

I led Leila through the glass doors.

Then the agonising airport wait began.

There were moments we laughed, and I tried to be strong, and then there were moments I couldn't be strong any longer, and my eyes produced more tears than I knew were possible.

How could I have so many tears?

Where was all this water coming from?

Why was the floor white?

"Let's have coffee?" said Leila, motioning to a small café right behind us.

"Okay," I replied quietly, standing up and pulling my suitcase over to the seating area. "Let me get these. What would you like?"

"Thank you, Abi. Hmm, Espresso. And you?"

"I will order cappuccino."

We sat. We waited, still surrounded by a web of silence, which was interrupted only by the occasional 'I love you', mixed with airport announcements, whilst we drank our coffee – our last coffee.

As painful and difficult as waiting was, it was nothing compared to that moment when my flight to London was announced, because, right at that moment, when I stood up from the bench we had been sat on, I swear my heart almost gave up beating. Leila stood up too, and I saw the fear and dread in her eyes. It was the first time I ever saw her look so lost and fearful, and this scared me even more. Yet, at the same time, I was so sure right then that, as much as I loved her, she loved me back.

"Come with me while I check in," I said, slowly and quietly, in a voice that portrayed every ounce of emptiness within me.

"I'm right here," she replied softly, as though drained of all energy and hope.

We waited in line just over a minute. There weren't many people checking in to this flight. I was up next. I pulled my suitcase closer to the desk and fiddled around nervously for my documents.

"Passport please?" said the lady, who was dressed in a navy-blue suit over a smart, white blouse.

I presented my passport and a folded print-out of my flight details. She typed something into a computer. She weighed my suitcase, which was then dispatched down the dark tunnel, which I could only imagine led to the aeroplane. She returned my passport, with my boarding card inside, and moved on to the next in line, a family of four.

"Gate number fifteen," she said, as I was leaving.

Leila and I walked towards the gate. She stayed close, holding my hand, and that was it: that was as far as Leila could go.

Right there and then, that bitter pain of loss hit me at full force, like a storm; it came just moments before our parting, as though the premature feeling was a warning – a sign that said 'don't do it', yet offered no way of staying.

"Leila, I'm scared," I whimpered softly, as we both looked up at the gate number and then down at the line that would separate us. "I love you so much. I don't want to lose you. You're my best friend. I need you."

"I love you too," was all she said.

We cried together, yet we were now apart. I had to go through to departures. I walked, like a corpse, almost. I could still see her from a distance as I left; she appeared so small and, though I could no longer see her features clearly, I knew she was doing exactly the same as me – she was crying.

Chapter Thirteen

When I was just eight years old, I witnessed my father's abuse towards my mother: raw, physical, violent abuse that engraved itself within me. I heard a blood-curdling scream that made the hairs on my arms stand upright; it was a significantly higher-pitched scream than it had been earlier, which caused me to crawl out from my hiding place behind a beige-coloured couch, only to see my mother lying on the floor in the doorway. My father had hold of the door and I watched, wide-eyed, as he slammed it, at full force, closed on her leg, again and again, as she screamed in pain: that raw, blood-curdling scream.

"Abi, look what your father's doing! Call the police! Call an ambulance!" she cried.

Her voice was distressed, yet manipulative at the same time, almost like when my sister and I were tell-tailing on each other, except she was an adult – she was supposed to be my mother.

I ran to the phone, stumbling over a smashed CD-player, stepping around an upturned chair, and tiptoeing unsteadily around broken ornaments, distorted fragments of something that was once whole.

"No, don't call them! It's just your mother!" shouted my father, angry yet pleading. "Look at her, she's on drugs again!" He pulled her up off the carpet, tearing her cardigan as he did so; he handled her like she was rubbish, a waste of oxygen. The sound of crying, material tearing, and the heavy thuds of limbs being knocked hard against something; these sounds engraved themselves within me.

I still hear these sounds today.

I was eight, and I had no idea whether she had over-medicated or not. I also had no idea what to do, or which parent to listen to. I just stood there, frightened, silent except for the occasional 'Mom!', though I don't even know why I kept calling her; she couldn't help me any more than my father could. *They* needed help... but I couldn't help them. I was eight years old and frightened.

My mother's leg was broken that day, and the police said my father had to stay away for a while. I had gone outside into the garden; I don't remember whether that was voluntarily, or if I had been ordered, but that's where I was left – outside in the garden for hours. I don't even recall where my sister was at this moment, yet we each witnessed our fair share of fights. Perhaps she wasn't living with us anymore; I remember she had been forced to leave the house when she was sixteen following quite an abusive fight, though can you call it a fight when only one person is acting on the other?

When I was eleven, I started to *act out*. I suppose I was in some way screaming for help in a silent, self-destructive way, that caused me both pain and further heartache. One time, I cut my face with a maths compass during break-time at school, and was confronted by my English teacher before the start of the next lesson. She asked me why I did it, but, despite wanting to be helped, I was suddenly fearful and reluctant to tell her. I was terrified and upset beyond words. Only my actions were capable of showing what I was feeling – the repeated scratches across my once innocent white skin. I was taken to the school nurse, and she told my mother what I had done, just as she had done the time I cut my arms and wrists. No further help came my way. When I looked back at that day, I wished the teachers at school had intervened; a girl of eleven self-harming is something that should have been dealt with and handled in a much more discreet and caring manner, yet it wasn't, and this was perhaps the first memory I have of the system failing me.

Not long after the self-harm incident, I began to develop an eating disorder; I over-ate and made myself sick, then other days I wouldn't eat anything at all, starving myself until my stomach ached with emptiness. But I didn't understand it; I didn't know why I was doing it, or what I was hoping to achieve. My mother found empty cans of food in my drawer that I had taken from the pantry to binge on and then make myself sick. She shouted at me once again, and made me feel humiliated and disgusted with my actions, but I couldn't stop it. I was spiralling out of control and being punished for it at the same time, yet all I knew was that I needed to do this, and I needed it to be private. Looking back, I suppose what I really needed was *help... and support*, yet I couldn't access it. At that age, I didn't know 'help' was even available; I didn't know I was worth helping – I didn't know *what* was available, and so I attempted suicide.

Sadly, I woke up.

When I reached sixteen and school came to an end, I couldn't take it anymore; the tiny ray of hope I received from my teachers was suddenly cut off, leaving me alone in a household filled with violence, neglect, and various kinds of abuse I did not understand. I ran away. Fear took over me one night; I barricaded my bedroom door shut for fear of an unwanted presence entering in the night. I was just too scared to go on living within a situation I could only describe as a slow and painful form of suicide; I feared abuse every day and *every night*. So, with every ounce of courage I could scrape together, I packed a few essentials, as much as my tiny frame could carry, and then snuck out of the house early one morning. I left a note, and told them not to look for me. I made my way to the bus station, suddenly filled with an energy that felt so foreign, yet so good. I hopped on a bright-red bus, and went to sit right at the back by the window, to get a clear view of what I was leaving, and the new place I was entering. Ironically, that particular day, as I sat on that bus surrounded by a small suitcase, a backpack, and several other passengers, was one of the happiest days I could recall. I felt a weight being lifted. All my fear melted away, and I knew then that travelling was my energy – my salvation in some way. Slowly and steadily, I began to build myself up, travelling, working in restaurants, and *being free*. I understood that there was something better out there, and I might be able to be a part of it. And, for a brief period, I was.

However, that's when the pattern began.

First, I travelled. This recharged my batteries until I felt normal. Then, I settled for a few months in a particular area, doing a job, making friends, and having fun. But then, after several months, I would begin to crumble; it was as though the past traumas caught up with me, inside my head, which already carried so many confusions, heartaches, and painful memories. I would have some episode, some kind of breakdown, and the humiliation of it would force me to leave… and then I would travel again. My batteries would be recharged until I felt normal enough to begin in a new place. I never managed to hold down a job for longer than six months; I was like a broken appliance, and that was just how long I could function until I broke again. The worst part, for me, was always the relationships that were formed – strong, intense, and *beautiful* relationships – which somehow shattered into a thousand tiny pieces each time. They shattered because of me. It was always my doing – something I did, yet did not, understand. The grieving that came as a result of those shattered relationships was unbearable, and always left deep scars behind; I grieved as though a death had taken place. It's safe to say that I battled day and night, year after year.

From an optimistic perspective, it was through the travelling and adventures that I did manage to meet the most amazing people, and make some beautiful memories that are still planted inside of me; they rest right beside the scars, and, in the same way as those scars, they are never forgotten. I don't know how I managed to survive for so long without professional help, with such a bizarre coping mechanism, but I did. I'm still here.

"I think that, deep down, you are a fighter. You are stronger than you realise," said Victoria, with a glimmer in her eyes that implied she was actually fascinated by my story.

"I don't feel very strong," I replied in a quiet voice. "I think I've just been running away for so long, and now I'm worn out."

"Abi – I believe you did what you had to, to survive. You've been through an awful lot of trauma, neglect, and abuse."

I smiled at her, because she made me feel like a survivor, if only for a moment.

During the periods when I was between jobs, I moved in with my sister, always temporarily, of course, sometimes just to 'recharge'. We seldom contacted our parents, apart from the exchange of Christmas cards, and birthdays too. Eventually, they gave up trying to have any kind of relationship with us too.

"Where are they now?" Victoria asked me thoughtfully. I told her that they remained in the same house we grew up in, in Tyne and Wear, and as far as I knew, they were still trapped in a vicious, never-ending cycle of fights, blame, and denial.

I pitied them, but I did so from afar, because I knew that I could never go back there, and, sadly, no part of me wanted to.

"Do you have anyone else in your family who you are close with?"

"I *did*," I replied.

Through all the neglect, abuse, and heartache growing up, I told her how it was my grandmother who was the one piece of normality, stability, and *love* in my life; she was well and truly a wonderful old lady. If only I could have seen her more often, lived with her, perhaps – how different my life might have been.

"She sounds very special." Victoria smiled. "You know, I noticed that your face lit up when you spoke about her just then. When did she pass away?"

"When I was a teenager. She was really special... amazing, actually."

Her death affected me a great deal; she died when I was around eighteen, but I always remembered that she was the most positive, gracious, and caring individual that existed throughout my childhood, and she showered both my sister and I with love, every single day. Only fragments of our abusive home life ever reached her ears, and she compensated for every bit of love our parents didn't give to us. She did this during the weekends we spent with her. They say a grandmother is irreplaceable; I know exactly what they mean. I remember the day I was in hospital, after undergoing an operation to remove my appendix; she arrived with a giant teddy bear, so soft and fluffy, and written on its two feet were the words: 'Hug Me'. She also brought with her a bunch of fresh, green grapes, and buckets upon buckets of joy, mixed with smiles, and sprinkled with laughter. Her laugh was like none I had heard before, and would capture the attention of everybody within a two-mile radius; it was loud, joyful, and infectious, just how laughter should be.

I remember how my grandmother had dresses in every colour and pattern, yet almost identical in style: knee-length, loose from the waist down, and fastened by a matching belt. I can still remember the green dress she wore more often than the others: emerald green with white spots. She always said green was her favourite colour, and anyone who knew her could easily identify this from her dresses, coats, and scarves. She even had a little brooch in the form of an owl, with tiny emerald green eyes that glistened in the sunlight on our way to church. I liked how each outing wouldn't be ready to begin until she had put one of her delicate, floral scarves over her hair, and fastened it underneath her chin. She really looked the part – like the devoted, classy grandmother that she was. I remember her perfume too: Blue Grass. It was the only perfume she ever purchased, and she wore it incessantly, modestly, and daily.

Something else about her that I remembered was how she always encouraged me to write poems, little stories, and keep diaries too, always praising my finished pieces, and boasting to her friends and neighbours about how her granddaughter was going to be a famous writer one day. For my sixteenth birthday, she bought me a beautifully-bound little diary with a flowery cover, and a little lock so nobody could read my secrets. Though, the funny thing about those locks and the keys that came with them was that they were all the same for every diary, therefore not quite so secure. But she didn't know that. My grandmother told me that writing a diary was like having a secret friend; that was also how she taught me about God when I was younger. She said I could use my diary to talk to him whenever I needed. My grandmother was always present in my life, until, all of a sudden, she was gone, and all I had left were the memories and that diary.

When I felt really lonely, I would write in my diary and pretend I was talking to my grandmother; I filled book after book after book with all I wished to say to her.

Dear Grandma,
Why did you go?
I'm still a child, and I need you so much and I didn't finish telling you how much I love you yet. I feel scared, and there is nobody I can tell. Come back, please. I don't want to live alone; I don't feel okay or strong enough anymore. Something isn't right, there is something wrong with me. I need you. You always made it look so simple, life, you made it look like such a beautiful gift and I don't know how to see it that way, not yet.
I miss you, Grandma. I miss you so much that it hurts.

These days, in quiet moments, I close my eyes and remember the steaming Sunday dinners she cooked, rich in flavour, and juicy, full of butter too. The creamy potatoes, the thick gravy with onions and tender beef; they were the most delicious Sunday dinners one could imagine. Her tight hugs, too, were equally sensational, as was the jolly laughter that always rang out at any given moment. I remember going to church with her on Sundays, the fish and chip shop on Saturdays, and the joy

165

of bath-times filled with a mountain of bubbles. Yes, a grandmother is definitely irreplaceable; my grandmother is irreplaceable. I fully believe that growing up without the support of a family, without any stability and of course, not feeling safe, are the key reasons I was so easily seduced into the relationship with Mohamed and Leila; I needed something to hold onto, to stop me from falling. I needed the stability of those walls around me. I think, subconsciously, I was always on the lookout for it, and, when I met Leila, she was strong, loving, and kind, so she seemed the right person to hold onto. Then Mohamed came along, and it was too late; I had already grown dependent on Leila, and would have agreed to anything to keep her. I *did* agree to anything.

I suddenly became aware that I was crying, and had been for a while, for my lap was damp where the tears had kept on falling whilst I had delivered the delightful tales of a woman I regarded my hero.

"Abi, I don't believe you have ever properly grieved for the losses in your life," said Victoria. "Do you think that it's safe to say you've been holding onto that pain all these years?"

I thought about her words and nodded my head. "Perhaps."

A quiet moment passed, where I sat with my thoughts, and so did she. I stared at the table in front of me, and she stared at me.

"Do you ever hear voices, or see things that nobody else sees?" she asked softly and thoughtfully, handing me a tissue.

"Thank you," I said taking it from her and drying my face.

I considered the question a moment, my eyes scanning the white walls until they stopped on the painting of the

166

green landscape that I had grown familiar with. In fact, each time I stared at it, another detail would suddenly jump out at me – one I perhaps hadn't noticed before. Sat on a patch of grass, near the blue stream that cut through the vast greenness, were several gentlemen fishing beneath the blue sky. They were painted so delicately, for they were barely bigger than my little fingernail, yet today, there they were, as clear and vivid as the moon in the clear night sky. It was a beautiful landscape, and I wished I could walk right on inside of it and dangle the tips of my toes into that stream. I forced myself to break away from my somewhat pleasant gaze, and rest my eyes on the lady before me, still considering her question. She waited patiently for me to answer, watching me as I had watched those fishermen.

"I don't think so... I have flashbacks, but they are just like memories." I looked at her, slightly confused and unsure.

I wasn't that crazy, was I?

She nodded her head, and then asked me about the session in which I had been gazing at the window, and how I had imagined that I saw Leila walking there.

"Was this a memory?" she asked me.

We both knew that it wasn't, but I could see she was urging me to look at things deeper, to try and understand on my own, minus her input.

"No," I responded quietly. "Maybe I am *slightly* delusional sometimes, I guess. I don't really know. It's a difficult question."

"It's okay, and you're right – it's not easy to determine this yourself. Everyone reacts differently to trauma, particularly when it is something too intense and complex for the brain to deal with; this can cause a kind of relapse from our normal self."

167

I felt ashamed.

What would my grandmother have made of this, if she had been alive?

Suddenly, it was not just shame I felt, but anger too. I was angry at my parents, for failing me. I was angry at the bullies who had tortured me every day but most of all I felt betrayed by the system, the one that's supposed to protect young children in vulnerable situations. The thing is, I have never been the kind of person to direct my anger at others, so it has always come back on me.

Had I just uncovered the root of my self-harm?

I closed my eyes and allowed my mind to wander. I knew what would happen, I knew where it would go, and I wanted it to go there.

We sat at the table, on two wooden stools, with several metal dishes in front of us. One contained foul; one had mixed salad; another held a generous pile of French fries; and the final one had scrambled egg, which Leila had made with butter. I broke a bite-sized piece from the round, flat bread in front of me, and so did Leila, and together we tucked into the food that was our breakfast: Egyptian food, my favourite.

"Mmm, the egg is so nice," she said, scooping it into the piece of bread.

"Yes, full of butter – you will give us both a heart-attack one day." I laughed.

Eshta was brushing himself against my feet, reminding me of his presence – not that I ever forgot about him. I took a little of the egg, dropped it on the floor, and watched as he lapped it up within a second.

"Abi! Now he will continue for more!"

I laughed as I walked to the kitchen to get him a plate, which I piled with egg, foul, and cheese.

"There you go, Eshta," I said, putting the plate down near my feet. "See, everybody is happy now."

Leila laughed, and threw a piece of bread at me. "What do you want to do today?"

"Hmm... we could go to the mall, near the Nile?" I suggested. "I want to buy some accessories."

"Okay." She smiled. "We could drink Asab too, from the shop outside."

"Yes! I miss Asab!" I replied excitedly.

Asab was a light-green liquid that came from sugar canes after they were pressed inside a large metal machine; it was very popular throughout Cairo, and very cheap too. It was my favourite drink, and Leila knew it always made me happy.

"Abi, what are you thinking about?" came Victoria's voice from within that tiny room with the laminate flooring and the blue-cushioned chair.

Chapter Fourteen

London, May 2015

Borderline Personality Disorder (BPD) is a serious mental illness where the individual is unable to manage their emotions efficiently, and they often experience them with a much higher intensity than is considered normal. People suffering from BPD struggle to maintain stable relationships, which can lead to depression, self-harm, and suicidal thoughts and attempts. They will often go to extreme lengths to hold onto these relationships, no matter how damaging or unhealthy they may be. It usually begins during adolescence, or early adulthood, and though individuals may function well in some situations, their private lives often suffer, leading to reckless behaviour, impulsive actions, and unstable relationships.

"I'm going to refer you on to a programme; it's called Dialectical Behaviour Therapy. It will be an eighteen-month course, so it will need your full commitment, but I believe this is exactly what you need," said Victoria Green, as she took a small sip from her coffee.

The delightful, robust aroma of it made its way across to me, bringing with it memories of early mornings in Cairo, stood on the balcony overlooking a busy street. I could almost feel the heat of Egypt as she handed me the booklet she had been holding onto (to explain the course in further detail.)

"You will find a lot of the information inside this book, which you can take home and have a read through, though we will discuss it in further detail in today's session."

"Okay," I said, taking it from her and browsing through the first page.

"You will need to be assessed first, and then we can go from there. How does that make you feel?"

"Okay, I guess. What exactly happens in this course; what is it for?"

"Well, it will go into great depth on how you are feeling, events that have happened in your past, and how you deal with them. It will help you to find healthier alternative coping strategies, and it's aimed at people who are often suicidal and self-harm."

"And the assessment? Will I need to explain everything again that I have already said to you?" I asked, feeling nervous and agitated at the very prospect of going through all this again.

"Yes, though the assessment itself will be over a shorter duration, just to be sure that this is the right therapy for you, and that you will benefit from it as opposed to something else. Is that okay with you?" she asked, studying my expression, looking for feelings and emotions that I might not be voicing.

I liked that she did that, for, over the duration of our weekly meetings, she had gotten to know me better, and could sense when there was something gnawing at my mind, even when I didn't say anything.

"Yes... but... eighteen months is quite a long time," I said quietly, as thoughts of Leila swam their way into my mind; I imagined her sat on the couch with a glass cup filled with dark tea, waiting for me in Cairo, where I had been not so long ago.

She was checking the time on her phone anxiously, and where was I? In London, having Dialectical Behaviour Therapy for eighteen months. Could I commit to that? Did I want to commit to that?

Would Leila wait that long for me?

I would wait ten years for her, but I doubted she'd wait for me. In fact, I was scared that she wouldn't, and didn't want to take the risk with the possibility of being right.

I missed her. I just wanted to hug her and feel that warmth, that closeness that I hadn't been able to feel since returning to the UK.

"It is," said Victoria, "but it will be worth it. Dialectical Behaviour Therapy has been known to be very affective in cases like yours."

"Okay – well, I will have a read of this booklet and find out a little more about it," I said, flicking through the pages briefly, though more for the benefit of my having just said that I would do so.

That night, I spoke with Leila and, once again, she urged me to return – pleaded with me, almost – and I felt at a loss, torn, and still damaged from the last time I had been there. Yet I was longing to see her again.

"I miss walking around Talaat Harb Square and Sherif Street at night-time with you," she said, planting inside of me images of colourful lights beaming from shop windows, and filling my ears with the belly dance music that so often streamed from a small radio or a TV.

Night-time in Cairo was often bursting with life and energy, for the air was cooler and more bearable minus the heat of the burning sun. It was still hot, of course; Cairo was always hot.

"I miss it when we would go and order pizza, and then sit on the floor in the room to eat it," I added, remembering how strange the pizzas had seemed to me compared to the English ones I was familiar with; they were made up of a thin, flaky pastry for the base (much like the one used for pasties and sausage rolls) and then the topping was the usual cheese and meat, tomatoes and olives, but mixed with egg, giving it an entirely different taste and texture.

"Me too. Hey, remember when we bought a kilo of zalabya... and I left them on the table, and you ate them all?" She laughed, bringing back the sweet memory and taste of those soft balls of light sponge, seeping with syrup, and reeking of sweet vanilla.

Those nights spent outdoors in Cairo were such wonderful memories, filled with grand display and rich culture – I missed them immensely.

"Come back to us," she said, just as she had said numerous times before.

I didn't speak, for I was still savouring the memory of the dusty streets, the smell of burning shisha, and the heat on the back of my neck. I opened my eyes, only to reveal that none of those sacred desires were anywhere to be seen. I was in the wrong place, and the panic of it suddenly caught up with me.

"OKAY!" I blurted out suddenly. "Okay."

"Okay what? You will come?" shrieked Leila, reflecting an excitement I felt inside.

"Yes," I said, this time in an almost-whisper, as though it no longer needed to be screeched or screamed; the simple whisper of that three-letter-word was enough.

Chapter Fifteen

Helen walked at a brisk pace through the street towards the Health Centre, a stack of files tucked under one arm, and her beige handbag in the other, swinging to and fro as she hurried. The birds made no sound as they soared above in the heavy clouds, and it seemed that no one was smiling as they passed on by. In fact, she couldn't even make out their features; everyone, everything, was a hazy blur, and despite there being so much noise and chaos around her, she heard none of it. Today, Helen was not accompanied by her younger sister, and this was what was wrong with the picture. Dark shadows below her eyes emphasised the exhaustion that consumed her, and a sorrowful look was now fixed on her normally so demure face – one that also held lines of worry from being awake all night. Breathing heavily, Helen switched from her brisk walking to a jog, and the force of the breeze caused water to form in her already tearful eyes. Gradually, small, sharp spatters of rain began falling from a sky that was dull and overcast, indicating an even harsher outcome in the coming hours.

She arrived at the centre, announcing to the receptionist that she needed to speak with Victoria Green, and that it was a matter of great urgency, though she needn't have said the words, for her appearance implied the exact same. Helen had not experienced such a feeling of panic in a long time, and the strangeness of it only unsettled her more. The large, circular clock in the reception ticked loudly and provocatively, as though mocking the stress and anxiety that whirred in the air above, whilst she sat there on the grey, plastic chair. Helen tried to control her rapid breathing, taking slower, deeper breaths, in through her nose and out through her mouth, though this was not easy considering the hurricane inside. Despite being a person that would read anything and everything, the cluster of magazines on a nearby table failed to captivate her attention today, and she almost burst into tears when she saw Victoria arrive through the side door.

"Helen," she said, with an air of surprise, mixed with a pleasantness that felt warm and welcoming. "Good morning. Would you like to follow me to my office?"

It was a rhetorical question, and she wasn't obliged to answer, though she did, with a slight nod of her head, standing and walking briskly towards her. Just as she had been on that very first meeting, Victoria was calm, collected, and polite, as she escorted her towards her office, though, after a few moments, there was an air of empathy, as she saw Helen's desperate state, and listened to her worries and concerns regarding her sister. She spoke quickly of events from their childhood, and Abi's odd behaviour even then.

"Please, Dr. Green, tell me; what is wrong with Abi?" she pleaded, with the highest level of desperation in her voice.

Victoria Green stopped along a narrow corridor, and led her into the room where she had often sat with Abi, listening to her tales and adventures, and the sadness, distress, and difficulties that had played their way throughout her life.

"Take a seat, Helen. Can I get you a cup of tea or coffee?" asked Victoria soothingly.

She smiled graciously.

"No, I'm okay, thank you."

Helen sat on the blue-cushioned seat, with Victoria opposite her, though before she could say anything more, she was suddenly distracted by the roses in a glass vase in front of her. They were displayed in the very centre of the wooden table, and the redness of those roses was so harsh against the white wall behind it that it took effort to draw her eyes away from them.

"I don't know what to do," she said, looking at Victoria with watery eyes.

"She's been making so much progress in our sessions. Her understanding of events and of herself is much improved compared to when I first met her."

"What's wrong with her? What's the cause of her... behaviour? Exactly how serious is all of this?"

She followed the array of questions with a series of deep breaths. Slowly but surely, Helen began to calm down, if only a little. Perhaps it was from being in Victoria's presence; it was as though the calm nature of this woman had somehow reflected and transferred into her own body.

"Your sister's behaviour was down to a number of things. It was a result of something called Post-Traumatic Stress Disorder, though I strongly believe that, underneath this, it is quite possible she has something called Borderline Personality Disorder," said Victoria, looking at Helen with a sympathetic, yet serious, expression written across her face, though the words themselves portrayed all the darker scenes of one of those many tragedy novels she had read. "So, it is vital that she receives the right help for this: a series of therapy sessions, plus medication, and to be around people who understand and can offer the right kind of support. She has dealt with a significant amount of trauma, and she no longer knows who she is. But, once again, I must express that she has come a long way."

It had been discussed, before any of the meetings had begun, that Victoria would have consent to be able to liaise with Helen regarding Abi's wellbeing. Abi had said it was absolutely fine, and hadn't seemed affected by the idea at all.

Helen sat there staring at Victoria, with wide eyes that were beginning to fill with water. She was still clutching her files from work in one hand, and her beige handbag in the other, while the words travelled through the air from Victoria's mouth to her own ears. There was a moment's silence between them, and that's when Victoria began to suspect something was very, very wrong.

"Has something happened, Helen?"

Helen remained silent.

It was like one of those slow-motion movies where there is a slight relapse in time; she was lost in a whirlpool of thoughts and worries, which caused a great stir inside, for she was never lost for words. In fact, it took her almost an entire minute to respond to Victoria's question. It just didn't feel real to her: her own sister, sick? No, it couldn't be. Especially now, when she had just found out that Abi had gone off travelling again.

"She's gone," she said finally, in a quiet voice, and with eyes that suggested her thoughts were far away.

"Where has she gone?"

"She went back to them... Cairo... she went back."

Another silence hung in the air between the two women – a silence filled with the noise of their own thoughts and concerns.

"Have you spoken to her?"

"No, and her phone is switched off. She left a note. Dr. Green, what will happen if she doesn't come back?"

There was another long and painful silence that hovered uncomfortably within the white-room in which they both sat and once again Helens' gaze was fixed on those red roses

"Well, I am hoping that, after all our sessions, Abi will realise that she needs to come back, and that the best support available to her is right here. I believe that Abi will struggle over there, as she did before, and she will see sense; she's a bright young woman, she's just lost right now."

"Do you really think she will come back?"

"Yes, I do, and you must remain positive and strong for when she does return. Please, continue to try to call her, and I will leave her a message too, on her mobile," said Victoria, in an assuring voice that was filled with empathy, and a touch of concern she hadn't intended to show. "Let her know that you are here for her, and that she has a safe place to come back to. I realise this is quite distressing for you, and she should never have gone off like that, but we have to respect that Abi is an adult, and we mustn't say or do anything to aggravate her just now."

Helen still felt uneasy, and, in need of some air, she stood up, paced the small room for a moment, and then sat down once again. Little did she realise that there was such symmetry between her and Abi at that moment, but Victoria saw it the instant Helen re-seated herself on the same blue-cushioned chair that Abi had always sat on while trying to make sense of all the situations that were occurring around her. Her neat, composed character that the world usually saw had transformed that morning into that of a nervous woman, who was filled with fear and confusion, just like her sister.

"Okay," she whispered finally. "You're right – we must remain hopeful, and all we can do right now is be here when she returns."

"I believe that she is just feeling desperate, and acting irrationally, which is likely to be due to an undiagnosed mental illness, but she will see sense. All you can do now is wait. Don't beat yourself up over this. She will be back soon."

Victoria took a deep breath, to calm her own sense of anxiety that was beginning to take hold of her, and held the box of tissues towards Helen, for she was crying now. Once again, the symmetry was apparent, as it was the same box that Abi had constantly drawn tissues from to wipe away her own tears. She saw their similarly-shaped faces, like perfect ovals, and their light-green eyes, which both glistened with a past full of neglect, abuse, and trauma

"Thank you," said Helen, wiping her eyes and blowing her nose. "I should go now, but thank you so much for speaking with me on such short notice... and reassuring me."

"If you would like to, stay a little longer... and have a cup of tea?" offered Victoria gently.

"That's very kind, but I should try to contact Abi again; I will keep you informed." And with that, she took one last glance at the red roses on the table, turned, and walked out of the door, slowly at first, as though in a trance, but then she sped up and walked, like a woman on a mission, down the corridor and out of the building.

The sound had returned to the street; the birds cheeped, and the cars honked their horns, whilst Helen took deep breaths, trying to remain calm, civilised, and like the woman she had worked so hard to become.

All of us are fighting the demons inside – that's what makes us the same. We're all trying to fit into this civilised world, trying to abide by the rules and ways of life, even though, on the inside, when it becomes too much, all we want to do is scream, go crazy, *explode*. Choosing to swallow those feelings is one of the hardest things. Yet, one of the bravest things would be to do the exact opposite, and to succumb to those feelings – let society try to adapt to *our* way, just as Abi had been trying to do. Helen suddenly saw her sister in a completely new light. Abi was such a strong young woman, who battled with society every day, and was still fighting to find her place in a world that was so unaccepting.

"Oh, Abi," she said quietly, as she walked briskly through the street.

Still sat at her desk, Victoria opened up her laptop, went straight to Abigail Hartley's file, and began to document the conversation that had just taken place, and the actions of the young woman whom she had listened to in great depth for the past few months. Since Helen's departure, Victoria had remained motionless for several minutes, digesting everything, and, at the same time, wishing there was something she could do to help. But she couldn't.

At the age of eighteen, Victoria Green had been sure that she wanted to become a psychiatrist, for the obvious reason of being able to help people suffering from mental health issues, but now, as she sat at her desk, looking across at that blue, cushioned chair where Abi had sat every week, she wondered whether she had helped this young woman at all. Deep breaths: in for four and out for seven.

"Come on, Abi; do the right thing," said Victoria quietly to herself.

Chapter Sixteen

Cairo, Tuesday 19th May 2015

I waited there on the sleek, marble floor, that glittered beneath artificial lighting, with eyes as wide and glossy as two china saucers, searching in the distance. Meanwhile, a cluster of women in headscarves and long flowing robes whizzed around me, pulling their children along in a hurry. I was no longer in Heathrow Airport – I had taken my six-hour flight with British Airways, and was now stood outside the vast open entrance of Duty Free in Cairo International Airport, wondering whether or not I was doing the right thing. I held my hands in front of me, watching them as they trembled without my consent. I took deep breaths whilst trying to steady them, wondering at the same time how my sister Helen would have taken the news, and hoping she would not be too angry or worried over my immediate departure. I had written a letter to her – a kind of apology for not saying goodbye, but explaining that I had had to leave. She would have read it by now, for sure. I checked my silver-strapped watch; yes, Helen would know now. I clutched my journal firmly in my right hand. My left hand was resting on the top of my blue suitcase, which stood beside me, tired and worn from use, just like me. I had been reading on the plane, and had read through some of my past entries, wondering how I would appear through the eyes of another – somebody who didn't know me, perhaps. Would they find me intriguing? Or would they simply suggest I see a doctor immediately? The pages had become heavily burdened with words, describing all my secret sabotages, my crazy obsessions, and the hurricane of moods that danced possessively around them, yet they were also mixed with an unexpected tenderness, which is what I had focused on throughout that flight. I'd read through my own exotic adventures overseas, and the intense relationships that had sprung from nowhere. Whether they had taken place in a small village in Italy, a colourful hostel in Miami, or the bridge overlooking the river Nile, they all had one thing in common: connecting with another. My heart swelled with emotion upon recapturing those moments; it made interesting reading, that's for sure. And, in some ways, that's what I wanted – to give somebody a story, to present somebody with a piece of myself and offer a lesson in life, at the same time as *connecting* with that person. Does that make sense?

There was a brief moment, whilst on that plane – and I mean brief – where I was actually contemplating throwing my diary in the rubbish, or leaving it in some random place, waiting to be picked up and read by somebody else. After all, I was here for a new start, and that cannot be achieved when one is holding onto the past. However, I did not dispose of it. In fact, after leaving the plane and entering the airport, I began browsing the rows upon rows of books and magazines I could see through shop windows, and I had another idea – an idea that, though quite far-fetched, suddenly seemed such a wonderfully exciting proposal. I might try to turn it into a book – a novel, perhaps. Maybe there was another young woman out there who had lived a life of similar struggles

– a woman who did not fully understand or respect herself. Somebody who had also spent their life climbing and falling, breaking and healing, and breaking again. Maybe *my book* could be her comfort on one of those dark days, rather than a path of self-destruction and turmoil; maybe my book could be a way of forming a connection with somebody. I remembered that day when my sister had brought the movie 'Into the Wild' home, and how the story had brought me a wave of comfort, satisfaction, and acceptance. I remembered how I'd felt when the boy needed to get away and set out on his own adventure, just as I had in some way tried to do. Yes, travelling by yourself can be a painfully, lonely venture at times, but it is also incredibly insightful, surprisingly educational, and it tests all of our limits. I felt this myself, I felt it today, as I stood in the airport, waiting for the next step of my journey to commence. In the movie, when the boy, Alexandra Supertramp (the name he called himself), wrote of similar thoughts and feelings in his journal, I'd felt a warm connection and sense of comfort that no person had ever been able to give me. I placed my journal into my grey rucksack, put the bag on my back, and resumed studying the swarm of people moving in and out of the airport as I so often did, analysing each and every one of them. One lady, to my left, dressed in a black gallabea and shimmering headscarf to match, was removing the wrapper from a chocolate bar for her small son. I noticed immediately that she was not Egyptian, but Saudi, from the way she wore her jet-black eye-liner, and the large quantity of jewellery dangling from her ears, neck, and hands. There was also the huge bulk under her headscarf that gave away her nationality, for Saudi women wear large hairclips, and additional scarves underneath the outer scarf, to create a largeness that, though it may sound odd, actually works, and looks incredibly glamorous. I was instantly reminded of the evenings I'd spent outside the Hilton Hotel, near the Nile, watching the array of Saudi women come and go; I smiled at the recollection. Not too far away from this woman was a gentleman in a beige suit, who was sat on a shiny, metal bench, reading a book, completely disengaged from everything going on around him. He was neither Saudi nor Egyptian. I tried to get a glimpse of the cover of his book, but could not. I watched. I waited. I analysed everything and everyone around me.

I waited for ten minutes for her, nervously glancing at my watch with every passing minute, then back to the moving crowd. It was the same airport in which we had said our last 'goodbye'. I just waited there. It was all I could do: wait in the hustle and bustle of the foreign arrivals, the continuous swarm of Chinese, Italian, Egyptian, and German-speaking groups and individuals whizzing past me. I read somewhere that 'waiting' is the word that best describes women from the East, as they 'wait', day in day out: first to transform from girl to woman, second to be proposed to by a man; they then wait for the wedding day, and the evening where the marriage is consummated; and then, they wait for their husband to come home from work, they wait for their first child to be born, they wait to be given instruction, – told what they can do and what they cannot – and then, they wait for God to decide when they will be freed from all of this waiting. Yes, my time in Egypt demonstrated to me this aspect of women's lives being solely based upon waiting, as the time passes by, whilst the men go on living. There are, of course, some women who live too – they work in pharmacies, hospitals, and shops – yet I *wait* for the day that the numbers of these strong and rare women increase from the current meagre minority. One time, when I was in Sharm El Sheikh, I came across a female security guard, Egyptian too. This surprised me, but not nearly as much as the woman's appearance – her deep voice, broad shoulders, and sleek, black hair stuck down with oil. Yes, she was one of a kind.

There were numerous security guards in Cairo Airport, all of them male and dressed in black, dotted here and there, bearing serious expressions upon their old and tired faces, eyeing everybody suspiciously as though each person entering the country were a potential criminal, a vicious terrorist, or a thief. I wondered what they thought of me – a young English woman in high-heeled shoes, stood by herself, journal in one hand, and suitcase beside her. I smiled at one of them, but did not receive anything in return, so I returned to scanning the crowds of people for the only face I did want to see. One woman, a very tall and beautiful woman, was causing quite a stir – well, more of a celebration, really. She was surrounded by other women with flashing cameras, beaming smiles, and joyous laughter. She was wearing a large, puffy, white wedding dress, with long sleeves, and her head was wrapped up in a white silk headscarf. It was obvious she was travelling to marry; what a wonderful surprise her soon-to-be husband would have. And suddenly, the colour white had an entirely new meaning to me; it was a colour of 'new beginnings'. My eyes darted around once more, eagerly trying to spot her in the ever-growing, ever-moving crowd. The atmosphere buzzed with foreign chatter, and echoing announcements of incoming flights. There were the familiar taxi drivers lingering by the glass doors, like hungry wolves preying on their next victim – a naïve tourist whom they could charge a hefty sum. And then I saw her, in the distance. Dressed in familiar dark

186

jeans, a pink, fitted top, and a grey, woollen scarf (for it was evening now and the air was a little cool) – it was Leila. She was walking towards me, slowly at first, unsure almost, but then, as our eyes met, I saw that she was almost running.

"ABI!" she called, her voice higher and happier than I had ever heard it, ringing out like the bells on the Christmas tree.

Tears welled up in my eyes, and my throat suddenly felt dry as I tried to call out to her.

"Leila," I choked, almost skipping towards her, though the ache in my muscles after such a long flight slowed me down, and my suitcase was suddenly too heavy to pull.

When she was just a foot away from me, I could see she was out of breath from the journey, from running up to greet me. Her face looked thin and malnourished, but her smile was as sweet and loving as ever.

"Leila!" I cried, suddenly regaining my voice. "You're here! Hi!" I threw my arms around her, completely abandoning my suitcase and bag. "I missed you. I missed you so much!"

The tears came and ran down my face uncontrollably, though mixed with joyful laughter.

"Me too," she said, her eyes filled with an emotion I hadn't seen for such a long time – perhaps not since I had first met her on that bridge overlooking the Nile, where she had taken my photo.

Oh, how fragrant was that memory: a beautiful scene that had not yet been tarnished or spoiled by fights. This – Leila and I –this was what true friendship was. It didn't matter about all the bad we had been through, for, when we saw each other again, we were just doused in an overwhelming happiness to be together again, after being miles apart not so long ago.

"Me too." She repeated the same words quietly, adding emphasis to her emotion, and almost crying now with a sense of happiness I think even she did not know she possessed.

"You look thin," I said to her pitifully, shaking my head, for I knew she didn't always take care of herself.

"Yes. Maybe." She shook her head as though it were merely a trivial matter on such a glorious occasion.

"I love you. Oh my God, I missed you so much!"

"Come here."

Leila hugged me again, this time even tighter than before, and, as I hugged her back, I knew I would never let go. Her eyes glistened beneath the lighting, and I knew mine were doing the same, for I could feel yet more water forming. I didn't even try to hold them back; in fact, I let them flow as naturally as the raindrops in England.

"Come on," I said, giving her hand a squeeze, and then turning to retrieve my suitcase. "Let's get out of here."

She stepped past me and took a hold of my suitcase. "Let me take it," she said, being the dutiful character she felt she needed to be.

In some ways, during those moments in and from the airport, I felt she was showing me how sorry she was for everything, and, once again, I felt the need to forgive this helpless woman before me, who I had always had so much love for. I would always do whatever I could just to stay with her; that's what love is – *sacrifice* – or, in my case, putting yourself through hell just to be with that one special person. Leila wasn't my girlfriend or partner, but she was my best friend, my family, and the person I knew I wanted to be with as I tried to make further sense of life once again. I looked at her; she was looking at me, smiling, as I waited for the feeling to arrive, the one that told me I was doing the right thing. I waited.

We stepped outside into the car park, which was covered by a heavy blanket of darkness; it was around one a.m. and a little cool, though it was a comfortable coolness, and one which I could bear. Leila summoned a taxi, then turned it away, after having a short argument in Arabic. I knew she was bartering a good price, though after the third taxi, I lost my patience and told her I would pay whatever he asked. Leila, however, was determined; I had always liked that about her.

The journey in the taxi to the centre of Cairo was quiet, yet pleasant, for we sat so close together, holding hands the entire way, pointing to various buildings and monuments that held some memory for us. We were always out walking in Cairo, and knew almost every area now. I felt relaxed, though, when the taxi came to a halt, a familiar feeling took over me. It was a feeling of apprehension – nothing too strong, but the overall familiarity of it unsettled me. As I stepped out from the taxi, a light gust of cool air wrapped itself around me. I inhaled the light fumes from the street, and then turned to help Leila, for she was already removing my suitcase from the car.

"Thank you," I said with a smile.

"You're welcome. Come on, let's go see the apartment! I hope you like it," said Leila excitedly, leading me through a concrete archway, up five stone steps that were covered in dust, and then through an array of rusty, iron bars into an elevator. It squeaked and rattled as it took us to floor five, then played a light melody as it came to a stop, and together we opened up its doors, which drowned out the music with their screeches and echoes as they closed again.

Leila was still smiling; she hadn't stopped, all the way from the airport.

"It's this one, just here," she whispered, inserting a large, metal key into an equally large, metal lock.

Dressed in dark jeans and a white t-shirt, there he was, waiting for us in the apartment they had both rented on my behalf. It was a beautiful apartment with two large bedrooms, a clean, well-equipped kitchen, and a carpeted living room, with a couch the colour of lavender. A familiar aroma of sweet, burning wood filled my nose as I entered that living room, which was coming from a burning incense-stick placed on the small, wooden coffee table. And there he sat, waiting with a smile as kind as a devoted husband. The musky scent of sandalwood that spiralled up from that little, brown stick brought back all those past memories of Egypt from what felt like so long ago (though in reality, it was only months that had passed by.) It conjured images of women in scarves pulling dark-haired children behind them through the streets, tall men in long, white gallabeas, sitting on wooden stools, smoking cigarettes, and others drinking dark tea in glass cups, with shisha burning by their sides.

"Welcome home," he said to me, standing, as though I was the Queen entering her palace for the first time.

"Hi, Mohamed," I said, putting my arms around him gently, inhaling his strong aftershave, that I recognised from previous intimacies.

He squeezed me tightly, as though he'd never let me go again. His hands moved slowly up and down my back, around my waist, until finally he had me caught in an uncomfortable embrace, which I felt I might never escape from. It was as though he was reclaiming his long-lost possession, and checking that everything that was once his remained intact. Already, I was beginning to feel that familiar sensation of being suffocated; my entire body was tense, like a cat when it's afraid, and that's exactly how I felt – *afraid*. Then, he held my face between his two enormous hands, and looked at me for a long, agonising moment, in which my stomach churned, and my eyes watered implacably, fighting back painful tears that had begun to sting my eyes. While a part of me inside was whimpering pitifully, like a desperate child in need of a mother's touch, I did my best to portray the feeling of love that was not there. I smiled, even though I did not feel like smiling; I hugged, even though I just wanted to grab Leila's hand and run; I continued everything I felt I needed to do, even though I desperately wanted to escape, to disappear into oblivion and beyond. We women are experts at making men believe that we feel something, even when sadly we don't, and I believe it is a talent we have been given to help us in the desperate situations we find ourselves trapped in. I wondered how many other women were living lives that they had resigned to, due to abandoned hope or merely desperation. He kissed me, and I knew I had succeeded, though somehow I did not feel the sense of fulfilment I had expected to feel upon returning to Cairo. I waited, still in his arms, for that *feeling* to arrive. I turned, releasing myself subtly from his clasp, and looked over at Leila. She was smiling. Her smile made me feel calm, if only for an instant.